GHOSTS

and Other Chthonic Macabres

Jana Begovic

Anna Blauveldt

Summer Breeze

Jim Davies

Codi Jeffreys

George Foster

Matthew Lalonde

Allan McCarville

Emma Schuster

Sara Scally

Michel Weatherall

Also available from Broken Keys Publishing

Symphonies of Horror:
Inspirational Tales by H. P. Lovecraft: The Symbiot Appendum

Thin Places: The Ottawan Anthology
(Winner of the Faces of Ottawa 2021 Book of the Year Award)

Love & Catastrophē Poetrē
(Winner of the Faces of Ottawa 2022 Book of the Year Award)

Sadness of the Siren, *by Samantha Underhill*

Missing the Exit, *by Michael Adubato*

Little Dragon, *by Jana Begovic*
Poisonous Whispers, *by Jana Begovic*

The Leavetaking, *by Anna Blauveldt* – Coming Soon!
Kat and the Meanies, *by Anna Blauveldt* – Coming Soon!

Titles by Michel Weatherall:
The Symbiot 30th Anniversary: The Nadia Edition
Necropolis
The Refuse Chronicles
The Symbiot Trilogy Box-Set

Ngaro's Sojourney

A Dark Corner of My Soul

Broken Keys Publishing & Press
Ottawa, Ontario

Broken Keys Publishing & Press

- *CommunityVotes Ottawa 2022 Best Printer Award (Broken Keys Publishing)*
- *Winner of the 2020-22 Faces of Ottawa Awards Best Publisher/Publishing House*
- *Winner of the 2022 Faces of Ottawa Awards for Book of the Year,* Love & Catastrophē Poetrē
- *Winner of the 2021 Faces of Ottawa Awards for Book of the Year,* Thin Places: The Ottawan Anthology
- *Nominated in the 2020 Faces of Ottawa Awards in the category of Book of the Year for The Symbiot 30th Anniversary, The Nadia Edition*
- *Winner of the CPACT-NCR 2021 Best Publisher Award*
- *2019 CPACT Awards Nominee for Small Business Excellence (Broken Keys Publishing)*

Blackburn Manor © 2022 by Allan McCarville
Demon Hunter © 2022 by Allan McCarville
The Forgotten Dress © 2022 by Jana Begovic
Harvest Festival © 2022 by Anna Blauveldt
Beautiful Killer © 2022 by Summer Breeze
Dream Eater © 2022 by Summer Breeze
Framed © 2022 by Codi Jeffreys
The Folly © 2022 by George Foster
The Drink © 2022 by Jim Davies
iWitness © 2022 by Matthew Lalonde
The Masked Cotillion © 2022 by Emma Schuster
The Last House on Macalister Street © 2022 by Sara Scally
Spirits of Strife © 2022 by Matthew Lalonde
Monsters © 2022 by Michel Weatherall
Running Water © 2022 by Michel Weatherall

All rights reserved

Cover photograph used with permission and licencing agreement with JJWenzeliMages © 2022
https://www.jjwenzelimages.com/
Cover Model: Mylee Batista

Published October 2022
First Printing

No part of this book may be used or reproduced, scanned, distributed in any printed or electronic form in any manner whatsoever without the prior written permission except in the case of brief quotations embodied in reviews.
Published by Broken Keys Publishing
brokenkeypublishing@gmail.com

www.brokenkeyspublishing.com

Blackburn Manor
by Allan McCarville

Lightning flashed across the dark horizon, followed by the subtle rumble of distant thunder. A summer storm was making its way down the Ottawa Valley as dusk journeyed into night.

The large mansion's ominous shadow loomed over me and I felt a fleeting sense of unease. I didn't know it at the time, but the disquiet I felt was a premonition that my life was about to change forever.

Two stories high, constructed from locally quarried limestone, the mansion was an imposing solid square structure. Vines had crawled their way up the face of the house, reaching almost to the eaves of the tiled roof, where a pair of chimneys were perched at opposite ends. A wide step led from the driveway up to an oak door that was flanked by two ornamental porch lights. Four large windows dominated the front of the mansion's lower level, two on each side of the door. Light shone out from one of the lower-level windows, the remainder, including the upper story windows, were shrouded in darkness.

Even in the fading light I could tell that Blackburn Manor looked to be in good repair despite its age, thus confirming my belief that the Blackburn family was indeed wealthy. It took serious money to maintain a centuries old house of this size.

I was here in response to a call for help from the manor's current owner, Jessica Blackburn, who planned to turn the manor into a bed and breakfast. She had just inherited the property from her grandfather, Samuel Blackburn, who had suddenly passed away a few weeks earlier. Heart attack from what I'd been told.

Jessica and I had attended university together, and for a brief period, I guess we could have been considered "an item." However, after graduation we drifted apart, our relationship unable to survive the difference in our social status. At least, that's what I told myself. I would never admit the truth, that real reason for our split had more to do with me and how I made my living. Let's just say I was not a model citizen.

So, I was rather surprised when Jessica called me one day, telling me she needed my help.

After receiving Jessica's call, since I knew little about the estate, I had googled Blackburn Manor. I had learned that it had been built back in 1840, and had been in the Blackburn family ever since. The Blackburns had made their initial fortune in lumber, then had expanded into other areas, not all of which would be considered legal.

That didn't trouble me; the things I did were not always legal.

I took my bag out of the trunk of my car and climbed the steps towards the front door. The porch lights came on as I approached, a woman I didn't recognize opening the door before I even reached it.

"Mr. Wilson?" she asked. Her voice quavered slightly. She seemed nervous.

"Yes," I replied.

"I'm the house keeper, Mrs. Dorothy Thacker," said the woman by way of introduction. "We were expecting you. Ms. Blackburn is waiting for you in the study." She stepped aside so that I could enter the foyer.

"Follow me," she instructed, closing the door.

I did as I was told, my gaze studying both the housekeeper and my surroundings as she led me down a wide carpeted hallway.

I followed Mrs. Thacker along the oak panelled hall, glancing up at portraits and photographs of men, women, even families, that hung at regular intervals. I guessed they were images of presumably now deceased members of the Blackburn family, judging from their attire. My guess was that the most recent portrait, which was actually an enlarged photograph of a man, was taken in the mid 1960's.

We reached an open door on the left. I stepped into the room: a desk occupied the centre of the room, with a fireplace situated on one of the walls, and a couple of armchairs were arranged in front of the fireplace. A woman who had been sitting at the desk stood as I entered.

Jessica Blackburn was a few years younger than me, and it had been almost ten years since we last saw each other. I remembered how pretty she was, but I was shocked at her appearance. I've seen recovering addicts who looked better.

"Jack," she greeted. "I wasn't sure you would come."

I placed my bag on the floor and nodded in acknowledgement. "Why wouldn't I come?"

Jessica didn't answer my question. She glanced over my shoulder to where the housekeeper was hovering.

"That will be all for tonight, Dorothy," she said. "There's a storm approaching. Maybe you should head home before it hits."

The woman nodded, obviously relieved. "Thank you, Ms. Blackburn." She cast a nervous glance at me then hurried away. That woman was frightened.

"What's going on, Jessica?" I asked. "You said you needed my help with a problem, but you didn't want to talk about the problem over the phone. Your housekeeper is scared."

Jessica shook her head. "No, Jack. Not scared; terrified."

"Scared of what?" I repeated.

"Not what, who," she replied. She pointed to the armchairs. "You better have a seat."

Jessica plucked at her jeans, looking furtively around the room before turning her attention back to me. "Grandfather told me some things about this house, things that have been happening. Since I've moved in after Grandfather's death, those same things have been happening. I know you're not going to believe me, Jack, but I've always had the ability to sense the presence of spirits."

"What?" I cried incredulously. Jessica had always been different, but I would never have thought that she was delusional. "Come on, Jessica. There's no such things as ghosts."

Jessica went to the desk and sat down. The surface of the desk was covered with papers, books and an open laptop. She picked up a piece of paper and handed it to me. "Read this," she directed.

It was a photocopy of a newspaper clipping dated the 14th of July 1848. I frowned as I read the text.

> *Jasper Collins hanged. Jasper Collins was hanged yesterday at the Carleton County Gaol. Collins was found guilty last month of the murder of Beatrice Blackburn. Collins denied his culpability, and showed no remorse for his crimes. Patrick Shaw, who is wanted*

for the theft of a number of valuables from the Blackburn estate, is still missing.

I frowned in puzzlement and looked up at Jessica. "What's this about?"

Jessica chewed her lower lip before replying. "I think either Beatrice Blackburn or Jasper Collins is haunting this house," she stated.

I shook my head. "Come on, Jessica. That's ridiculous."

Suddenly, the room was illuminated with a flash of light that burst through the windows, followed almost immediately by a peel of thunder that reverberated throughout the house.

A loud crash sounded on the floor above.

Then the lights went out.

Jessica screamed. I jumped.

For a few long seconds the only sound I could hear was my heart hammering in my chest.

"Jack?" squeaked Jessica.

"I'm here," I breathed hoarsely. I didn't realize I was holding my breath.

The lights flickered back to life. I wasn't sure who was more relieved, her or me.

"The house has a backup generator that kicks in automatically when the power goes off," Jessica informed me.

I took a moment to allow my heart rate to get back to normal, telling myself that the clap of thunder, the lights going out, and the sound of something falling upstairs, just happened to coincide with Jessica's statement that the house was haunted.

"I'm going upstairs to see what caused that crash," I said. "You wait here."

"Like hell I'm staying here alone," she hissed.

"Okay, but stay behind me," I ordered. I wasn't being chivalrous; having someone watching my back was a matter of self-preservation.

We cautiously made our way up the stairs.

"There's a light switch on your left," Jessica informed me when we reached the top of the stairs.

I flicked it on, and several wall mounted lights illuminated the upper hall revealing a number of doors on each side of the hall. "What's up here?" I asked.

"The master bedroom is the last door on the right," Jessica replied, indicating down the hallway to my left. "There's also a bathroom, three more bedrooms, and a storage room."

I glanced to my right and saw a small table lying on its side, split in two. Obviously, that was the source of the crash we heard. What was a mystery, was how it was damaged in the first place? I knew one thing; the table didn't do this to itself.

Someone had to be up here.

With Jessica on my heels, I searched each room, even the storage room, but found no one. I had no explanation, but was not yet willing to buy into Jessica's belief that a ghost was wandering about the mansion.

"There's no one here," stated Jessica. "Like I said, strange things have been happening."

I couldn't argue that what we had seen and heard wasn't strange, but I was certain there was a logical explanation. There had to be, right?

"Strange, yes. But that doesn't mean there isn't a logical explanation. Why are you so insistent that there's a supernatural explanation?" I asked her.

"Come back down to the study and I'll explain," she said. She turned and headed back down the stairs, and, after another quick look up and down the hallway, I followed.

We returned to the study where Jessica went to a side board and took out a decanter containing an amber coloured liquid, and two glasses. "Whiskey?" she asked, holding up the decanter. "My grandfather kept a supply of excellent Irish whiskey."

"Please," I accepted. Jessica poured both of us a healthy measure.

I took a sip, the whiskey doing wonders to calm my nerves. "Okay," I said to Jessica. "Look, I don't want to question your so called *ability*, but is there any real evidence that this place is haunted?"

Jessica indicated the various documents and books piled on the desk. "I did sense a presence when I first arrived, but it was Grandfather who thought the manor was haunted," she replied. "I read through all this material," she explained, "and coupled with some strange things that happened lately, I came to the same conclusion. From what I've read in the various diaries, great-grandfather was also suspicious that something was going on, although he wasn't as categoric about it as Grandfather."

Her eyes narrowed. "How about you read it all and tell me if I'm off base?" she challenged.

I looked at the top of the desk and shook my head. I had no interest in pouring over all that material. "How about giving me a synopsis," I suggested.

Jessica took a sip of her whiskey then leaned back in her chair. "Okay," she began. "First off, Beatrice, whose maiden name was Watson, was married to my great-great Grandfather, Edgar Blackburn. She was Edgar's second wife, his first died giving birth to Joseph Blackburn, my great Grandfather. She was much younger than Edgar, and from what I've read, it seems that she and Jasper Collins were having an affair."

"Really?" I found the idea of Jessica's ancestor's promiscuity intriguing and couldn't help but smile.

"It was only later that the affair came to light," continued Jessica. "I came across a few letters that Beatrice had written to a sister, and in those letters, she hinted rather strongly about her feelings for the estate's groom, one Jasper Collins. I've found some old letters written by Edgar, and he alludes to the fact that Beatrice was unfaithful to him."

"So, he knew his wife was cheating?" I asked.

"It would seem so," Jessica responded. "However, it's not clear when he came to that conclusion."

"The fact that he might have been aware of his wife's infidelity is definitely a motive for murder," I said. It was my experience that in murder cases involving infidelity, the perpetrator was almost always the surviving partner.

Jessica nodded. "It is," she concurred. "However, in reading over the few surviving accounts of the trial, the rumoured affair never came up. On top of that, Edgar was not at home when the murder occurred."

"I presume his alibi was confirmed?" I knew that investigative procedures in the mid-nineteenth century were vastly different from modern police techniques, especially since the use of forensics as an investigative tool had yet to come into its own. Nevertheless, I was certain ascertaining and confirming alibis was standard procedure, even back then.

"It was," Jessica confirmed. "Edgar was in Carleton Place for a meeting with his business partner. He didn't get back to Ottawa until the next day."

"Okay, so Collins was arrested, convicted and hung. I presume there had to be some evidence against him."

"There was," said Jessica. She selected a couple of pages from the pile on the desk and quicky skimmed then. "According to this," she waved the papers in front of her face, "They found Beatrice's favourite silver pendant and chain hidden in Collin's quarters, along with over a hundred Pounds Sterling. It's believed that Collins was in the process of robbing the house but was interrupted by Beatrice. He strangled her to keep her quiet."

"Strangled?" I questioned.

"That's how the coroner said she died," said Jessica. "Collins was supposedly in the process of robbing the manor. Beatrice caught them, and he killed her. That was the theory at the time."

I looked at the copy of the newspaper article. "And just who was Patrick Shaw?" I asked.

"Oh. He was the boot boy," she answered.

"Boot boy?" I had no idea what a boot boy was.

"Boot boy," repeated Jessica. "His main duty was to clean and shine the boots of the family and household staff, as well as any other tasks, like running messages."

"Just how old was this boot boy?" I wondered.

"Not sure of his exact age," admitted Jessica. "He was an orphan indentured to Edgar Blackburn until he came of age.

He was eight when he was indentured, and had been indentured for about three years when Beatrice was killed."

"So, Patrick Shaw was eleven or so, and he disappeared," I noted. "Did they believe that he was in league with Collins?"

"The theory is that the boy was an accomplice," said Jessica. Her eyebrows creased into a thoughtful frown. "Do you think it could be Shaw who actually killed Beatrice?"

I shook my head. "No. Strangling someone takes strength. I doubt an eleven-year-old would be strong enough." I was mentally reviewing the information Jessica provided. Something was gnawing at the back of my mind, but I just couldn't put my finger on what it was. "What was stolen?"

Jessica picked up a notebook. "Grandfather made a list." She flipped a few pages then read, "Well, there was that pendant, plus a broach, a diamond ring, diamond earrings and a gold necklace. Oh, some cash was missing too. A hundred and twenty-five Pounds Sterling."

"And the only thing recovered was that pendant?" I noted.

"Just the pendant, and the cash that was found in Collins quarters," she confirmed.

"So, the rest of the jewellery was never found?" I asked with a thoughtful frown.

"Guess not," she replied with a shrug. She noticed the look on my face. "That mean anything?"

"Don't know," I answered. "Anyone who steals jewellery would need to sell it. For a thief, jewellery has no value sitting in their pocket. They have to off-load it. That means knowing who to sell it too. So, if Collins stole the jewellery, he had to have someone lined up to buy it from him."

"That makes sense," Jessica agreed.

"So, if he stole the jewellery, why did he keep the pendant?" I wondered. "Was it worth a lot of money?"

"Several hundred Pounds Sterling," said Jessica. "That was a lot of money in those days. Maybe he kept it as a keepsake?" she suggested.

"I doubt it," I said. "If he only wooed Beatrice in order to rob the house, there'd be no sentimental value for him." Something wasn't making any sense. "How soon after she was killed was Collins arrested?"

"Within a day," Jessica answered.

"Okay. All this family history is interesting, but you still haven't told me anything to suggest this place is haunted. You mentioned strange events. Just what type of strange events are we talking about?" I asked.

"According to the notes and journals written by my grandfather and great-grandfather, things began to happen during Collins's trial," Jessica informed me. "Things like candles going out. Doors opening and closing on their own, odd noises, things being moved."

"But no one admitted to actually seeing a ghost?" I commented, arching my eyebrows and doing my best not to smirk.

Jessica glared at me. "Can you tell me what we experienced upstairs a few minutes ago wasn't strange?"

I had to admit she was right. It was strange, but I wasn't yet ready to admit that it was a paranormal event of some sort.

"A breeze will blow out a candle," I told her. "This is an old house, so there's bound to be drafts, and an old house settling would explain any creaks and groans. A door that is no longer hanging properly will not latch and could open on its own."

"True," she concurred. "But tables don't fall to pieces on their own," she stated, pointing to the ceiling above us. "Plus, I sense a presence in this house. An angry presence."

There had to be a logical explanation, but I just couldn't come up with one. *Ghosts aren't real* I told myself.

Suddenly, a photographic flash lit up the room, a crack of thunder rattled the windows, followed by the unmistakable sound of footsteps running up the stairs.

I sprinted from the study with Jessica on my heels. I bounded up the stairs two steps at a time. I reached the top just in time to see the door to the master bedroom swing shut. I charged down the hall, shouldered the door open before it latched, and burst into the room, my hand snapping the light switch.

No one was there.

Jessica raced into the room behind me. "Where did they go?" she asked.

I didn't reply. I looked around, even dropped to my knees to look under the bed. Nothing.

The room was large by modern standards, with two windows: one directly across from where I was standing in the doorway, the other on my left. Typical for a corner room. Looking out the window, in the distance I could see a dark ribbon that I realized was the Ottawa River. On the wall to my right was a closed door, presumably a closet. I signalled

Jessica to stay behind me, took hold of the doorknob, then wrenched it open.

The closet was empty. It wasn't very wide, and there were narrow shelves on the wall at each end. From their size, I presumed that once upon a time they held shoes. Victorian houses were notorious for their small closets; this closet was large by Victorian standards.

"You heard someone on the stairs too, didn't you?" Jessica's comment was more of a statement than a question.

I couldn't deny it.

"Are you ready to believe me now?" she asked, giving me the 'I told you so' stare.

"No," I snapped. My denial was spoken with far more conviction than I actually felt. I wasn't ready to agree with Jessica. Admitting that the house was, indeed, haunted, would be an admission that ghosts existed. It would be an admission that humans were more than mere biological machines. It would mean admitting there was an afterlife. Such an admission would upset the foundations of my belief system. I just wasn't ready to go there.

Whoever had run up the stairs, couldn't walk through the wall, therefore there had to be a hidden door. Given the age of this place, and in view of the family's occasional criminal undertakings, I was convinced there was a secret passage or something.

"What makes you so sure this feeling you have is due to Beatrice or Collins being present?" I asked as I ran my hands along the interior walls of the closet. Whoever the intruder was, he must have somehow gotten out through the closet. That was more believable than Jessica's insistence that the ghost of Beatrice Blackburn or Jasper Collins lingered in the hallways.

"It's difficult to explain," she replied. "However, there's an angry spirit in this house and it must be one of them. Spirits only linger for a couple of very specific reasons. Quite often, it's unfinished business resulting from sudden death. I'm leaning towards the spirit being Beatrice as she actually died in this house."

"So, you're saying that Beatrice - and I'm not buying into the belief that she's here," I added hurriedly, "has unfinished business because she died, or rather was murdered."

"Precisely," stated Jessica. "It could be that she's angry at Collins, or, possibly, it wasn't Collins who killed her. She would want justice. If Collins was innocent, it could be his spirit that's haunting the house. That's the main reason I asked you here. I believe confirming who killed Beatrice will allow the spirit to cross over."

I was about to tell Jessica what I thought about her ridiculous idea to investigate a crime committed a hundred and seventy years ago when, suddenly, three loud knocks echoed throughout the room. I jumped backward out of the closet, almost colliding with Jessica.

"What the hell?" I turned a full 360 degrees in a vain attempt to identify the source of the knocking.

"That's the spirit knocking," said Jessica.

"No," I hissed in denial. "Not possible."

Inside the closet there was a click, followed by an ominous creaking noise, a noise I recognized as long neglected hinges opening under protest. I leaned forward to peer into the closet, and with the light from the bedroom, it looked like the shelving unit on my right had swung outwards.

Looked like my theory about a hidden door wasn't wrong after all.

"That didn't open on its own," Jessica whispered in my ear. She was looking over my shoulder, but was lingering outside the closet. I recalled that she was claustrophobic.

"Did you know about this?" I asked, pointing to the opening.

She shook her head. "No," she replied. "I've not found any reference to any secret rooms or passages in any of the information from either grandfather or great-grandfather."

I took a tentative step into the closet and used the light from my mobile phone to examine the opening. I pushed, and the hidden door squealed in protest as I forced it wider. The light revealed a square space, about four feet by four. It was empty, and the layer of dust and abundant cobwebs was evidence that no one had been in this space for a very long time. At first, I thought it was just empty space, then I noticed a small ring in the floor. Given the accumulation of dust, I couldn't tell if the ring was part of a trap door or served some other purpose.

I passed my phone to Jessica and took hold of the ring and yanked with all my strength. Aside from almost dislocating my shoulder, nothing happened. "Not a trap door then," I remarked, turning to Jessica.

Out of nowhere a cold breeze swept past, strong enough to ruffle my hair. It created a small wind devil, churning up dust and dirt, a funnel appearing over the ring. Centred at the top of the funnel was a blue orb of light. It plunged downwards, passing through the floor.

Suddenly, the floor boards exploded upwards.

I hit the floor, pulling Jessica down with me, covering her with my body.

The dust settled and I stood shakily, then reached down and helped Jessica up off the floor. The light from my phone did its best to pierce the floating dust and I could see a square hole. It seems there *was* a trap door after all.

"Either Beatrice or Collins wanted us to find that opening," remarked Jessica. "Now do you believe me?"

"Yes," I said reluctantly between fits of coughing brought on by the dust. I could no longer deny my own senses. I cautiously approached the hole and looked into the darkness. I could make out boards nailed across some posts, forming a makeshift ladder. I shone my light down into the abyss, but it didn't have the strength to cut through the dust to expose what was at the bottom – assuming there was one.

"We need to go down there," Jessica restated.

"We need a better light," I countered. "And we need to make sure that makeshift ladder is safe. Lord only knows how long those boards have been there. They could be rotten."

"I have a flashlight in my room," Jessica advised me. She slipped away, and, much to my dismay, returned a few minutes later with a large LED flashlight. I really didn't want to journey down that ladder into the unknown, but it was either head into the hole or look like a total wimp in front of Jessica.

I shone the light down and gingerly placed one foot on the ladder. I cautiously put weight on the rung, and when it didn't break, slowly began my descent. When my head cleared the hole, I stopped and swept a beam of light towards the bottom. To my relief, there was one.

"What do you see?" asked Jessica, who was on her knees, looking down at me.

"Looks like a shaft that goes down to the cellar," I answered her. "I can see what looks like a clay floor." I continued my way down, testing each rung, which made for a slow, but safer descent.

I reached the bottom of the ladder without incident, except for being ambushed by spider webs every few seconds. Stepping away from the ladder, I took in my surroundings that were illuminated by the flashlight's strong beam.

"Jessica," I called. "You better get down here."

"I'm here," she said, startling me. I hadn't heard her follow me down the ladder. "Oh my," she breathed in awe, looking around.

We were in a room, which I guessed was located under the garden at the back of the house. It wasn't a large room, but it held a desk, a bed, and a table with a couple of wooden chairs. A couple of heavy beams, braced by a couple of sturdy posts, supported the ceiling. There was an old oil lamp on the desk, and a candelabra in the centre of the table. A wine rack was located on the wall next to the ladder, and an archway marked the entrance to a tunnel.

"What is this place?" murmured Jessica. Then she half smiled. "I wonder if this is a secret love nest. Maybe this is where Beatrice and Jasper had their little rendezvous?"

It was certainly a cozy little spot, albeit slightly musty. I made my way to the desk where several mouldy papers had disintegrated. Whatever was written on those pages would never be known. What had caught my attention, however, was a tin box. I tried to open it, but it was locked, but, given its weight, there was definitely something inside.

"Think you can get it open?" asked Jessica, looking over my shoulder.

"If I can find something to force it," I said. "Might damage the box though."

Jessica shrugged. I took that as permission to force the box open. I found an old letter opener on the desk but wanted to check out the drawers, just in case there was a key. Unfortunately, the wood had swelled. I was willing to bet those drawers had not been opened this century.

It took some effort, but the letter opener did the trick. "Holy shit," was all I could say when I looked at the contents. Light from the flashlight sparkled as it reflected off precious stones. The gold and silver might have tarnished with time, but the precious stones had not lost their brilliance.

I had no doubt this was the stolen jewellery.

There was more. A leather-bound journal was under the jewellery. I picked it up, and carefully opened it. The leather was cracked and the pages within were a little brittle, but had not yet disintegrated. Being careful not to damage the pages, I gently began to peruse the contents.

"What?" demanded Jessica when she saw the grin on my face.

"You were right about this being a love nest," I told her. "However, it wasn't Beatrice and Jasper's nest, it was Edgar's."

Jessica's eyes widened in surprise. I was about to pass over the book but noticed a paper that had been tucked inside the book at the end. I took it out before handing the journal to Jessica. It was a letter dated the 14th of September, 1848. I read it as Jessica began to read about her great great-grandfather's mistresses.

"Oh, dear," I muttered after reading the letter. I carefully set it down, hoping that I hadn't damaged the letter by handling it. "Jessica. When did your great great-grandfather die?" I asked.

"Huh?" Jessica was so engrossed with the journal it took an effort to pry herself away. "Oh. It was a few months after Collins was executed," she informed me. "He was thrown from his horse." She saw the look on my face. "Why?"

"You might want to read that," I said. "Handle it carefully," I added, earning myself a scowl.

Jessica's jaw dropped as she read the letter. She looked up at me, then focussed her attention back to the letter, reading it again.

"William Carlsberg was Edgar's business partner, wasn't he?" I asked her.

Jessica nodded. "Yes," she sighed. "This letter explains a lot."

The letter was addressed to Edgar Blackburn's business partner, one William Carlsberg. In the letter, Edgar was advising Carlsberg that he was going to wait a few more months before selling the jewellery, then he would send Carlsberg his half of the money. The man also commented that he had eliminated the witness who could place him in Ottawa the night of Beatrice's murder, rather than in Carleton Place.

"It would seem that your great great-grandfather and William Carlsberg were partners in Beatrice's murder," I said. "My guess is that Edgar killed Beatrice in a fit of rage, then made a deal with Carlsberg. Carlsberg provided the alibi in exchange for half the profits from the sale of Beatrice's jewellery. From the date on the letter, I think Edgar was killed by the fall from his horse before he had a chance to post this letter."

"And Carlsberg couldn't very well demand his money from Edgar's estate without admitting that he lied about Edgar being in Carleton Place," observed Jessica.

"The fact that Beatrice was strangled had bothered me," I admitted. "Strangling someone takes effort. It's very personal. Not how an intruder would kill someone who happened upon them during a robbery."

"So, Jasper Collins was actually innocent," stated Jessica. "That would explain….."

She got no further. The room filled with a blue glow that coalesced into an orb. The orb circled the room, then darted through the arch into the tunnel where it hovered.

"I think it wants us to follow it," said Jessica.

I was startled to realize that, like Jessica, I could now sense an emotion stemming from the spirit that lingered just inside the entrance to the tunnel. Maybe it was because having finally accepted the existence of ghosts, the inhibitions that had previously blocked my ability to sense their presence had vanished.

I didn't sense anger or rage; I sensed impatience. I glanced at Jessica who, like me, didn't seem to feel threatened by the spirit. I shrugged and we headed into the tunnel as the orb lead the way.

The tunnel sloped gently downwards, and I tried to visualize approximately where we were in relation to the manor. The hidden room was at the back of the house, and extended into the garden, flowers and shrubs growing just a few feet above it. I guessed we were still under the garden.

"We're going deeper, aren't we?" said Jessica, glancing nervously about, her claustrophobia kicking in.

"Not really," I reassured her. "The land at the back of the house slopes downward. I think we're still only a few feet underground."

I shone the light about the tunnel, noting that the passage, including the arched ceiling, was constructed of brick. I said nothing to Jessica, but I really hoped that the fact the brick was intact after more than a century and a half meant that it would remain intact; at least until we were out of the passageway.

The orb we had been following stopped. When it did, it's light expanded to reveal a door blocking the tunnel. Then the orb vanished through it.

I stepped closer to the door, examining it carefully with the flashlight. It had originally been constructed to fit the tunnel, but its wooden planks had begun to rot. The hinges and door latch were made of iron, and given the amount of rust, I assumed the door would not be easy to open.

I leaned against the door while pressing on the latch as hard as I could. The door latch was unyielding, but the wood where I pressed my shoulder splintered. A solid kick completed the destruction and I shone the light into the space beyond.

We could go no further. A few paces on the other side of the door, the tunnel had collapsed. However, that was not the most startling revelation.

Partially buried under the rubble was a body, or rather, the skeletal remains of an unknown individual.

"I guess we had better call the police," I said.

* * *

Eight months have now passed since the night that Jessica and I had encountered the angry spirit that had been haunting Blackburn Manor. Jessica and I are now partners in the Blackburn Bed and Breakfast. As for our personal partnership, that's a work in progress, but I'm hopeful.

I rested one hand against the fireplace mantle, the other held a glass of whisky. I gazed into the crackling fire before looking up at the pocket knife that was sitting in a holder on top of the mantle. It had been discovered in the remnants of the jacket found with the skeletal remains. The blade had been cleaned of rust, and the old wooden handle had been oiled slightly to prevent further deterioration.

The type of knife a boy would have possessed in the middle of the nineteenth century.

The remains were determined to be those of a boy aged somewhere between ten and twelve, who had died about 170 years ago. The authorities could not positively identify who it was, but Jessica and I knew it was Patrick Shaw. We arranged for a quiet funeral service, and that's the name on the headstone.

There was some reluctance by the authorities to reopen the case against Jasper Collins. Afterall, the man was long dead, and nothing could be done to alter the outcome of his trial. Nevertheless, Jessica hired a lawyer and eventually Collins was granted a posthumous exoneration.

A meaningless gesture? Perhaps. At least the truth has been established. The truth has to count for something, doesn't it?

I looked over to Jessica who was seated at the desk, sipping a glass of wine, and raised my glass. Tomorrow, we will be welcoming our first guests.

"To a prosperous future," I toasted.

Jessica grinned and raised her own glass. "To a prosperous partnership," she countered. I didn't know if she was referring to our business or personal partnership. She set her glass on the desk. "But now for some ground rules," she said.

"Patrick!" she called.

Jessica and I determined that it was neither Beatrice nor Collins who had been haunting the mansion, but rather the spirit of young Patrick Shaw. The medical examiner who had examined the remains found striations on the ribs, concluding therefore that Patrick had been stabbed to death. Naturally, after so many years it was almost impossible to prove anything, but the police surmised that young Patrick must have witnessed Edgar Blackburn murder Beatrice, or the boy had seen the man around the house when he was allegedly in Carleton Place. Either way, Edgar Blackburn had to silence the boy.

It was little wonder that the boy's ghost was pissed off.

There was no doubt that Edgar had been the one to kill Beatrice, but it was not known if Carlsberg was an accessory before or after the fact. That was a moot point now.

"Patrick!" she called again; this time impatience coloured her voice.

A small orb of light appeared in front of the desk, then it materialized into the translucent figure of a young boy. The boy had appeared to us several times since that night, yet I still found it slightly unnerving, even though the hostility he had originally displayed had long since disappeared. I have no idea why he was still here. I'm new to this consorting with ghosts thing, but Jessica says she's not surprised the boy is lingering.

The boy glanced at his knife, then at me before turning to Jessica.

Jessica smiled warmly at the boy. "Tomorrow our first guests are arriving," she told him.

Patrick nodded.

"I don't want you scaring them," she warned, frowning slightly.

I wasn't sure, but I could have sworn I saw disappointment in the boy's demeanour. He held up his hand, a small space between his finger and thumb.

Jessica was better than I at interpreting Patrick's gestures. He hadn't actually spoken to us, I don't know if he can, but communication was not really an obstacle. At least not for Jessica.

"Okay," relented Jessica. "But just little things. You can move things or turn lights on and off, but keep yourself hidden. We don't want guests having heart attacks. It's bad for business." She glanced up at me before adding with a grin, "Although a little haunting might actually be good for business."

Patrick soundlessly clapped his hands, then coalesced into an orb of light, circled the room, then vanished. I sensed his happiness, a happiness I shared when I looked at Jessica.

I think I'm beginning to understood why Patrick was still around. Like me, he was searching for happiness. Ultimately, aren't we all? But happiness is not something you find; happiness is something that awakens inside you. It comes with appreciating and accepting what you have.

I studied Jessica thoughtfully and couldn't suppress a contented smile.

My happiness had awakened.

The Drink
by Jim Davies

On the deck of the ship Brenda found a handsome guy named Phil, but only a few minutes into the conversation he started to look too appetizing for her to concentrate.

"If you listen to the lyrics; I mean if you read them," he was talking about some band, "they're so cryptic and just... profound..." She found his enthusiasm infectious, but not enough to actually go and listen to it.

"I've heard they're good." It was a lame response. She could not keep her mind on the conversation, what with the smell of his blood beneath his skin. AB, she was pretty sure. She heard his heartbeat. Or at least, she thought she could hear it. It was faint, dreamlike. Could she actually be hearing his heartbeat?

His hair was long, and a bit of it was caught on his eyelash. Every time he blinked she watched, hoped, it would break loose. Blink. Nope. Phil was oblivious, like some people are when eating cereal with a drop of milk on their lip. "Gotta check their latest album. Amazing." He was talking again. What had she missed? Didn't matter. She glanced around; they were alone on the deck. She went for his throat.

She approached and his eyes widened. Must have thought she was making a pass at him. He even stepped back, but she took him by the arms and leaned her head in. He turned his lips to hers, but she opened her mouth and put it on the side of his throat, fangs extending.

Get it right, Brenda. You'd think with a degree in biology she'd have no problem getting the right carotid, but she'd botched it yesterday, leaving somebody screaming and with almost no blood flow.

So much for a state school education.

Phil tensed as her fangs went in, and a small moan escaped his lips. Then he said "ow." The blood started to enter her mouth. Yum. Definitely AB. Nothing like warm, living blood cells to make you feel like you're not dead. "Ow!" he said, louder, and then pushed her hard.

Brenda was stronger than she was when she'd been alive, but, it turned out, still not as strong as Phil. Her grip, with her teeth and hands, came loose, tearing the skin of his neck. She tried to retract her fangs before he saw them, but oh the smell of blood was everywhere now and she was still a bit lost in a drinking reverie. "The hell?" Phil said, and tried to stop the glorious bleeding with his hand.

Shit. Brenda had only been a vampire a few days before she'd got on this stupid night cruise. Ted had told her not to do it. She'd insisted it would be fun and here she was, realizing that it was a pretty stupid idea after all. Now Phil's eyes widened as his mind tried to make sense of the vampire in front of him.

Not good.

She lunged at him, but he must have taken judo or something, because he got her into some kind of throw. She landed hard on her back before she knew what was happening to her. Now it was her turn: "Ow."

No more Ms. Nice Vampire. She sprang up, noting, thankfully, that you can't get the wind knocked out of you if you don't breathe. She reached for him; they grappled briefly, and she found herself thrown again. In the air.

More air?

In the ocean.

Whenever Brenda had imagined falling off a medium-sized cruise ship at night, it seemed really scary: falling about ten feet and landing hard onto cold, dark water, and then being under, in her clothing, not being able to breathe, freezing, totally disoriented. Now that it was really happening she felt most of these things, but came to her senses rather more quickly because, as a vampire, the cold wasn't so bad, nor the fall, nor the inability to breathe. Aside from talking she hadn't breathed since she'd died - when was that, Tuesday? It was only Saturday.

She'd learned to swim when she was alive, so she kicked off her heels and swam to the surface. The ship was already at least fifty feet away and disappearing rapidly into the darkness. She tried for a minute to swim after it, but it was clearly too fast, and looked to be half a mile away in no time.

Fuck. She turned around and saw the land behind her. It looked to be a few miles away, but she also knew that distances looked different on the water. She started swimming back to shore. She felt her clothes were slowing her down, and she thought of taking them off, but didn't want to be naked when she got out.

* * *

Two hours of swimming the land seemed no closer. She was tired, but not out of breath. It was pure muscle ache. Do vampires have lactic acid buildup? Felt like it. The night was so silent. She took a break and began to sink. What limited air she had in her lungs kept her quasi-buoyant, but not like a living body.

Most of all she was hungry. Very hungry. She'd already been hungry when she'd lunged for that black belt Phil, and only got the tiniest bit of his blood. Very unsatisfying, like taking a single bite of a hot fudge sundae, her favorite food. Or was. Didn't sound very good now. Ted said food would make her vomit. She'd been bulimic when she was sixteen. Didn't want to start that shit again.

She kept swimming. She sang songs to herself, just for something to do; that killed a few hours. Turns out her catalogue was shorter than she'd expected, and by the time she was singing "Happy Birthday to You" she was bored out of her mind and the land looked only a little closer.

What was more unsettling? That the sky was getting lighter, or her buoyancy, or lack of it?

She hadn't felt sunlight since she was alive, but according to Ted it caused your skin to burst into flame. How does it feel, she'd asked. "Like you've burst into flame." *Ah.*

When she paused, took a break, she ever so slowly began to sink; the deep unknown dark beneath calling to her.

It started to look like dawn would arrive before she got to land. Brenda panicked, thrashing about and screaming into the empty morning. After a few minutes she calmed herself. She licked the salt water off her lips and smoothed her hair. God, she was hungry.

If she dove, submerged, could she suck the blood of a fish? She poked her head under the water and could barely see anything. Not that she thought she'd be able to catch one. As a vampire she was fast, but not fish-in-water fast. She swam down as far as she could, but did not reach bottom, and, frankly, it was scary down there. She wanted to just lie on the bottom and sleep the day away. She coveted what little air she held in her lungs. At least a neutral buoyancy.

Hungry and feeling like a complete idiot, she swam faster toward shore.

The sun was coming up and she'd never been so anxious in her life. When dawn finally broke, a gentle, lovely ray of sunlight played upon her head. It seared her cheek. Her forehead caught fire, then her eyelids. The pain was enormous. All this happened in the second it took her to get her head below water.

The salt water stung but ultimately made her head feel better. She could not close her left eye, because of a missing eyelid. Very disturbing, but thank God things like this hurt less when you're undead.

She found herself exerting a rather lot of energy just to stay buoyant. Now with her head completely submerged, she kept swimming in what she was pretty sure was the direction of land. She didn't dare come up for a peek through. She used the sun's location as a guide. But should she? Maybe she should dive, sink away from the sun, into the inky blackness below?

The other unfortunate consequence of the sunrise was that the top several feet of ocean was getting brighter, and slowly burning her skin. She found she was getting a bad sunburn, even underwater. She swam deeper, but had to swim at a downward angle to stay low enough and keep moving toward shore. The dark deep called to her, its voice both tantalizing and terrifying.

She recalled playing in the pool as a child, and how hard it was to sink an air-filled ball. The farther down you tried to press it, the harder it wanted to come up. *Great.* But she didn't need to breathe. Lungs full, lungs empty, matter little. She could dive to the beckoning depths, simply exhale, giving up what little dead breath remained.

Now she wanted to swim completely under the water. After an hour she realized she had to swim deeper and deeper as the sun rose and the light penetrated farther down. She didn't need to breath, but her old instincts were still there, putting her mind in a state of near-panic. The deep dark beckoned.

At one point Brenda was so exhausted she just stopped swimming, just for a moment, to rest.

She must have been closer to shore now she figured, and as such the water must not have been as deep. She tried again to swim to the bottom. Maybe there would be something there she could hold on to.

She could scarcely see her hands in front of her, and soon they were ghostly blue shapes as she went down and down.

Her hands hit sand, and then struggled along the bottom, looking for some seaweed or something to hold onto.

Think Brenda...

She dug into the sand and tried to bury herself. Exhausted now, she used her last surge of adrenaline to scoop the ocean bottom. Some of the sand covered her, but its weight wasn't enough to hold her down. She knew she had to exhale.

Then, in the corner of her eye, she spotted something darker. She swam to it and felt a large rock. She wrapped her arms around it and held tight.

The grip took strength, but not as much as swimming did. She tried to calm down, but the only tool in her toolbox was deep breathing, which wasn't an option for many reasons. She counted down from a hundred....then again.

When could she safely go back to the surface? She looked up and saw blackness.

If she could hold on longer....but her energy was long gone.

A thought bubbled up from the depths of her mind. A desperate thought.

The weariness in her arms fully entered her consciousness. As she relaxed her grip, ever so briefly resting, again, her body began to float upwards toward what she now knew must be the blistering light of day.

She exhaled, purging the final remains of any oxygen in her lungs, emptying them completely, allowing the dark ocean water to fill them, any hope of her buoyancy gone.

Her undying body settled to the ocean floor, the crushing pressure of the depth like a soothing blanket of darkness. Famished, crying, her hope faded as the ocean above her brightened Her fear of the unknown above outweighed her fear of the deep darkness.

The Folly
by George H Foster

I hadn't intended to die that morning three years ago. To be honest, I had not intended to die anytime soon, either!

Oh, before going any further I should introduce myself, I am Brian Baines, late of Exxon Mobil Corporation, a very big corporate name in the oil, gas, and energy business.

I was a steam turbine engineer by trade; and yes, steam turbines do still exist, even after one hundred and thirty-three years, although today's versions are infinitely more efficient than old Charlie Parsons pure reaction machine.

My career spanned forty-three years, from graduating from Cal Tech in 1972 to retiring in 2019. Most of that time was spent in oil and LNG plants throughout the far and middle east.

I lost my wife and seven-year old daughter in a road accident fifteen years ago when I was overseas. I never married again, it didn't seem right somehow. But then, who knew there was more than one kind of family?

Not having a family meant that I did OK money-wise. Not that I wouldn't give up every last cent if it would bring them back. If it were not for having to send a constant 38% of my income to Uncle Sam, despite not having stepped foot in the USA for more than a couple of weeks a year, I would now be filthy rich. As it is, I'm as rich as I want to be at this stage of my life.

I used a good portion of my richness to buy an 1850 Victorian pile with 18 acres of land in the country, about five miles outside of Dublin, Central Georgia. It cost me $760,000, and I figured I would need at least another $100,000 to fix it up, but what the heck, I had the time and the money as they say.

The house stole my heart the first time I saw her. Six bedrooms, five baths, and 6,000 square feet. She was constructed using Georgia heart pine and boasted original woodwork, stained glass, and wonderful doors with Eastlake hardware. She also came fully furnished with mid-1800 period pieces, and although dilapidated to a fairly large extent, I could immediately move in and use her as my home.

She has a very private lot too. A driveway runs almost a mile up to the house off of the Old River Road, and to the rear, nothing but forest, all of which I own, leading eventually to the Oconee River.

I had inherited the services of a housemaid, Mary, from the previous owners. Mary comes and takes care of me on Mondays, Wednesdays, and Fridays. To be honest, although 60 years old Mary keeps the house running smoothly without any help from me; she really is a blessing.

On the eventful Sunday I want to tell you about, I had risen at 0700, brewed coffee, boiled two eggs, toasted a couple of slices of whole wheat bread, and moved out onto the back balcony to enjoy my breakfast.

It was early May, before the main body of bugs arrived, although their advance guard was well ensconced and causing a little irritation.

As I enjoyed my frugal spread and looked out over the garden, I spied a stone tower peeking over the trees some distance into the woods. There was no tower mentioned in the house listing and despite our discussing the property several times the agent, and indeed the house inspector had not mentioned a tower on the property.

Now, my eyes are not as good as they were. I had been meaning to go to see my doctor for a while. I had read up on cataracts and that is what I thought I had. Like looking through a raft of cells! However, I could see reasonably well in the growing light.

The top of the tower tantalizingly appeared and disappeared as the early morning tree top mist wafted this way and that in a gentle breeze. I could not get a solid sighting of the structure, but my fleeting impression was one of a round edifice, faintly Gothic, in a slate-gray colour.

The sun began to burn off the mist and as it did, paradoxically, the image of the structure faded to nothing in the brightening light.

I shook my head, *"silly old fool,"* I thought. *"Seeing castles in the clouds now are we?"*

Even so, I had nothing to do, a pleasant by-product of retirement, so I pulled on my well-worn, unlaced, work boots and headed into the tree-line.

* * *

I found a narrow path that had frequent patches of flat broken stone. I walked carefully, I didn't need a sprained ankle, although subsequent events proved that to be a low-bar anxiety. There were remnants of broken-down split-rail fencing on either side of the path. Evidence perhaps that the path had once led to somewhere other than deeper into the woods.

The sun was up, and the woods were dappled with shafts of light. The air was warm and smelled of fresh leaves, oakmoss and amber.

I had only gone a hundred yards or so when I came to a clearing. The ground was made up of dead leaves, sheet moss and crab grass. A couple of tree branches lay where they had fallen. The clearing was roughly circular, and I surmised that someone had spent some time keeping it clear in the past. There were plenty of trees close to the perimeter so they should have seeded some saplings over the years. However, no seedlings or sprouts disrupted the strangely flat surface.

Across the space there was what looked like a portion of a wooden stairway leaning against a tree. That piqued my curiosity, it looked incongruous, out of place, so I headed across the dell to investigate.

I took three paces and the planet tilted sideways. My legs crashed through what I now know was the rotten flooring of the tower. I tried to bend forward and reach out for the illusion of solid ground. I fell onto my chest which knocked the wind out of me but had the presence of mind to dig my fingers into the moss which held momentarily and then began to tear away from the rotten wood. in my panic I swung my legs back to try to gain some purchase on the wall behind me. That just hastened the tearing of the moss. I frantically kicked and swung my legs around seeking purchase until the moss finally let go and I slipped backward screaming into the darkness.

I don't remember any of the fall. I do remember floating upward through a dark sea of pain and finally coming to, lying on my back, with my right ankle screaming a sawtooth song of agony.

My ribs hurt like a son-of-a-gun and there was also a searing pain in my head. I reached up and explored gently through my hair. I touched a large lump, and my fingers came away wet and sticky with blood.

I was prostrate, so I tried to maneuver into a sitting position. When I moved my right leg, the pain from my wrecked ankle shot through me with the intensity of a hundred scalding needles. I almost swooned and resolved never to move again!

Looking around and upward I took stock. I sat against the rough stone wall of a circular space. Above my head, some fifteen feet or so, the hole I had made allowed sunlight to stream down through the disturbed dust and shed light on me and a small area around me. The floor was flagstones covered in a smooth layer of dust and dirt. Reaching halfway up the wall opposite to me was the bottom portion of a stairway. The other half I suspected; was the part I had seen above that had lured me across the clearing.

I was in trouble. I didn't know just how much but the more I thought about it the clearer it became. Mary was the only person on Earth who knew I was at home. It was mid-morning on Sunday, and she would not show up until mid-morning on Monday. I had no cell phone and I reasoned no-one had any business on my private property.

I could not ignore the pain from my ankle any longer. Gingerly I drew my ruined foot toward me by pulling on my pants. Inch by inch, despite the fiery torture, I pulled it into the light. My boot was still on. But that only helped to show just how bad it was. The skin was not broken but my foot inclined twenty degrees away from my leg with my ankle as the pivot point. That area was already swollen and an ugly blueish black. It was going to get worse, that I knew.

Although only fifteen feet separated me from safety it might as well have been five hundred. I wasn't going to climb out of here. I doubted I could even if the steps yonder had been intact.

My saviour would have to be Mary. Twenty-four hours then. That is if she even noticed I was missing. Could I last 72 hours? Mary would not suspect anything tomorrow, I often go to town of a morning, but she would not then be back until Wednesday.

I remembered from my days working in the Libyan desert that the lack of fluids was going to get me. I would be dead within three days if I was fit, which I had to admit I wasn't. Someone had to find me on Tuesday at the latest, or I had to find water. Neither option seemed very likely.

* * *

I spent the rest of the day alternately cursing my stupidness and lamenting the imminent loss of my life. The space warmed up uncomfortably and throughout the day my body began to dry out. By nightfall I was as dehydrated as I had ever been, but I knew this was just a harbinger of the shitshow to come.

I had a fitful night to say the least. My prison, for that is what it was, even though only 150 yards from my backdoor, stayed eerily quiet that whole night. I could hear the rustlings of small and medium-large animals above me. At one point there was enough moonlight for me to see a bobcat gazing down at me through the opening I had made. I gazed back not actually knowing if that is what I should do. She must have smelled my blood, but after a bit she growled at me and turned and disappeared.

Another thing that should have given me pause but went over my dumb head, happened about an hour later. I had been drifting in and out of sleep and dreaming of laying in a snow-covered field. It was cold, so very cold! I woke up suddenly, shivering to beat the band. My breath steamed in the frigid air. My teeth chattering, I pulled myself into as tight a bundle as I could manage. One thought bounced around in my head, it never got this cold in Georgia in springtime, even though it was night, this was…. unnatural.

The cold gradually dissipated and the normal early morning warmth crept in. I slept again.

When I awoke, I noticed something new. As I mentioned before, my eyes are not as good as they could be, and for a moment I thought they were playing tricks, but as the morning lightened, I made out a disturbance in the dust running from the centre of the space over to the remnants of the stairs. Two parallel lines scuffed into the dust - looking an awful lot like *footprints*. That got my attention!

The Bobcat. She would have no problem climbing down here and back up. But how did she get out without going through the hole I had made? I was lying right beneath it! The idea frightened me in no small measure. A fit man with a weapon would have no problem scaring off even a full-grown bobcat, but I had nothing. Still, I was a two-hundred-pound man and not a small rodent, her normal prey.

My mind settled in on that, she could smell my blood and knew I was hurt but not by how much. She would be cautious and probably wait until I was dead or close to it before she got braver. I relaxed thinking that, but how wrong I was!

I had been awake for a while after sunup when I imagined I could smell damp. Where there was damp there was water, I figured. It seemed to emanate from my right. I took stock again. To move will be agony, it will also take me away from the hole above me. Rightly or wrongly, I trusted that gap to be my saviour, I was reluctant to move.

I waited with the pain in my ruined ankle - now a sharp stab with every beat of my heart - for the sun to rise and to traverse the blue cloudless sky. The pathway from house meandered from east to west so I figured once the sun had cleared my house and the trees, I would be able to guesstimate the passage of time by the angle of the shaft of sunlight through the hole I had made. When it reached where I estimated it meant it was around 10am, I mustered all my energy and screamed *MAAAAARRRYYY HELP MEEEEE.*

I stopped and listened, willing and praying that I would hear her call out but the rustling of the breeze in the trees mocked me.

Three more times I tried calling. Each time my voice got softer as my thirst began to take a toll on my ability to speak let alone cry out. I finally slumped back against the wall and drifted into fitful and pain laden sleep.

My hopes that Mary would be my saviour faded as the sunray moved across the wall of my prison, slowly showing me the passing of the day. I was weakening fast, if I didn't get some fluids into me, I certainly was not going to last until Wednesday.

In the evening, before dark, I decided to chance the journey to where I thought water might be.

I had no means to splint my foot, so I began the agonizing journey, pulling my body straight with my elbows, and then reaching down to pull my foot the couple of inches that gave me. Each time I did that the pain knifed through me and I had to stay still breathing deeply, until the torture subsided.

In this fashion, and keeping my face close to the wall, I finally found some wet stone. It was covered in mold which I scraped away to reveal a crack in the mortar that oozed water.

I licked the wall.

It wasn't going to be enough. I did get some sour tasting liquid on my tongue that gave me a shred of hope, but despite digging at the mortar until my fingers bled, there was no more than a film of water.

I lamented the lack of even a basic tool to dig between the stones to where there surely had to be an accumulation of water. I had on track pants so not even a belt buckle to use as a tool.

The long night passed in the same way as the previous one, slowly and painfully. I dozed and woke intermittently, uncertain what was real and what was fantasy. I could feel myself getting weaker physically but also mentally. I wondered wryly what part of me would crack first.

The damp stone provided precious little comfort or fluid, just enough to prevent my tongue from swelling and cracking. The icy cold came again, inexplicable, and bizarre. It lasted about an hour and then the space around me slowly warmed up to normal early morning levels.

I dreamt a lot. Mostly about water, ice cold and delicious, but upon wakening the pain, abject discomfort and desperation returned, mocking me with their inevitability.

* * *

It was now Tuesday morning. I had been in the hole for about 44 hours and my chances of being found were close to zero. It had been almost 46 hours since I last drank some fluids, and that had been my morning coffee on Sunday.

The sun shone down through the cavity I had made. I scrutinized the wall and floor as the sunbeam advanced slowly across the space like a spotlight on a stage. It revealed nothing. Just dry, parched stone and earth and dust. The builders of this room had done a great job of waterproofing, darn their fastidiousness!

The heat of the day had passed but my prison was still very warm, and the thirst had taken on a malignancy all of its own. I was going to die, I was certain of it.

I drifted off again and awoke with the sun no longer beaming down from the hole I had made. My eyes adjusted to what my mom used to call dimpsy dark.

I sighed with despair, but before I could lapse into my painful world of self-sorrow, I spied a disturbance in the gloom on the far side of the room. I jumped and gasped as the pain caused by my movement tore through my ankle. Shaken, I stared at the area where I had sensed the motion.

My heart pounded painfully against my chest. The awareness of my predicament swept through me anew. Alone, unarmed, vulnerable, no hope of rescue.

Slowly at first and then more quickly the temperature in the room started to fall. I began to shiver uncontrollably. A lifetime of nightmares and horrors came unbidden into my thoughts and truth be told I whimpered. I'm sure if I wasn't so dehydrated, I would have wet myself.

I fixated on the place on the other side of the room. Despite the lack of sunlight, I could still make out the pattern of the stones making up the wall. Nothing stirred. Breathlessly I watched and waited, my heart still hammering.

As if emerging from the wall itself a small boy appeared and walked slowly toward me.

At first, he was ethereal, hollow, without substance. My mind reeled, frantically casting about for an explanation. Then I had it, he must have climbed down when I last passed out.

Thus, partially reassured I tried to speak but my tongue cleaved itself to the roof of my mouth, I could barely manage a strangled squeak.

The boy stopped and stood still looking steadily at me. Somehow, through the fading light I could pick out his details. He was wearing what seemed to be a gray soldier's uniform with a single line of buttons down the front of the jacket. His pants with a single red side-stripe were a little too long and pooled at his feet. *Scuffed footprints?* A yellow sash encircled his waist, and the cuffs of his jacket were a subdued red. On his head he wore a civil-war kepi type cap adorned with cross sabres. He carried a toy rifle, the kind with a spring-loaded ratchet that would make a bang when the trigger was pulled.

I tried to speak again but could only whisper *"help."* The effort or the trauma caused me to swoon again.

Only out for a minute, but when I came to the boy had moved. He now stood quietly across the room from me, looking at me with sombre eyes, and dare I say *pity*?

He moved a step or two laterally into the room and I realized he was pointing down at the base of the wall. He continued to look at me silently without an ounce of malice apparent on his face.

Deep breathing hurt my ribs but raggedly at first and then with more confidence the exercise worked its magic, and I began to calm down.

My mind started to explore the possibility that the boy was not real. A figment then? I was in bad shape both physically and mentally so that may well be the answer. But the kid was so well defined, could I imagine so much detail?

Slowly it dawned on me that I was in the company of a ghost. But curiously, the thought did not fill me with dread. Actually, now the initial shock had worn off I felt comforted.

If I had been visited by a ghost alone in the cosiness of my home, I would have stained my underpants. The idea that the world was not just the physical and science and facts would probably have scared me silly. That there was a supernatural for sure would have made me doubt my sanity and question reality.

I have read Poe, King, Lovecraft, Shirley Jackson, and others of course, and even though their genius had crafted a myriad of tales, there was always a sense of *sameness* about ghost stories. They all said that ghosts are the ultimate outsider, can never become one with the living. That alone makes them wretched and sad, they must feel so *forlorn!*

Despite all that, ghosts must have a reason to be here. A tragedy, a task, a quest, a message, to right a wrong? I chuckled despite my pain and my anxiety; I'm actually pondering the purpose of spirits. *Get a grip!*

I looked up at the boy. He hadn't moved. Still the steady pointing hand.

The lad wanted me to see something. Maybe the kid had been murdered and here was the evidence of the crime. Or buried over there was a lost family treasure, or the skeleton of a long-dead pet.

Getting there was going to be a horrendous trial by fire. I hoped it wouldn't be on account of a pile of bones or rags. I felt compelled to try though. As they courageously say, hope springs eternal. I set off.

In my world of anguish and pain I did not notice that my ghostly companion had left me. At about the half-way point I stopped and rested. His absence gave me a pang of regret. He may have been otherworldly, but he had been company and he made me feel safe. I continued the torturous crossing through the dirt and the dust.

As I drew closer to the wall, I could again smell wet stone and earth. This time though it was a fresh smell, a cold smell.

Ignoring the pain, I dragged myself more quickly to where the boy had pointed. He must be an angel I realized; he wasn't pointing at something for him but something for me.

About three inches above the floor a vertical segment of the mortar had fallen out from between two stones and water trickled out. Not much mind you. Trickle is not a valid unit of measure, but this volume would be enough to fill my mouth at least once in a matter of a minute or so. As long as it didn't stop it had the potential to save my life for now. I put my mouth down to the sliver of fluid and half licked and half sucked at the gap between the stones. The water, grainy, ice cold, with the most delicious flavour I had ever tasted, filled my mouth. I swallowed and looked at the wet fissure. The water had stopped flowing. I watched in desperation as the seconds ticked by, then it started trickling again. Jubilantly I repeated my effort and was rewarded with another mouthful, and then another. After 5 minutes I had drunk enough to feel the effect on my body as it rehydrated. I was going to live, for now.

I stayed close to the dribble of life-saving water. I began to feel stronger. That night I slept as opposed to passing out, and in my sleep, there were dreams.

I dreamt that I was with the boy. He was fair and small and lively. Blue eyes and a freckled face. We played hide-and-seek in a world of warmth and light and smells and the soft sounds of nature. I smiled in my slumber; I was happy.

Sometime in the night I awoke to see my new friend playing on the far side of the room. Although the night was pitch black, I could see him clearly. He *glowed*.

The vicious cold had not returned so I did not feel fear or even concern. I should have been babbling in fright for heavens sake! I was alone in the dead of night with a boy who was certainly departed. But it was as if I was numb, outside of all this, looking on, in a safe place.

Does everyone who meets a ghost eventually reconcile with the initial terror? Or was my ghost a special kind? One who meant no harm and therefore did not alert my primordial instincts.

I dozed again and woke with a horrific thought. I was dying! That was it. I was dying and the boy was my spirit guide. I'd heard of helper angles coming to earth to guide the newly dead to the afterlife. That must be it! My time is up, and the boy was waiting for me to kick off.

I spoke to him now that my tongue had gotten back to normal size and my throat had opened up. He didn't respond though. It was as if I wasn't there.

He can't communicate with me, I mused. When my body dies, he and I will be on the same plane, and he will come and guide me to the new place.

Shoot! As I said at the beginning of this narrative, I wasn't ready for that; the dehydration problem was solved but my ruined ankle hurting like a son-of-a-gun reminded me of something else. When the realization screamed unbidden into my mind it was like a punch in my face. Blood clots? Deep vein thrombosis? Are these things killers?

I gingerly examined my ankle. The thirst and then the boy had almost driven the pain from the wound from my mind. No longer, it was hot to the touch, and although not bleeding the swelling stretched my skin to a parchment-like state. I knew that the fluid build-up was my body trying to tackle infection. But what happens without treatment, will that fluid actually get into and poison my blood?

I pushed the thought to the back of my mind. I wasn't in immediate danger, for now anyway, thanks to my little soldier who was also a comfort to me. I lay back and watched him, my mind drifting in and out of focus.

Sometimes he marched up and down like a guardsman. Other times he played with different toys I couldn't quite see. At one point, for a good ten minutes he lay on his stomach and flicked through the pages of a book. I figured that in life, this was his space, his playroom.

From time to time, as I watched, the room yonder took on form. A bookshelf, a mirror, a rocking chair. All similar to period pieces I had in the house. I was looking into the past brought to me by this lifesaving youngster.

He was still there when the sun came up.

I waited anxiously for the sun-clock to indicate it was around ten and then I let out my best yell for Mary. Nothing. I tried again ten minutes or so later. Just the wind in the trees. Four more times I screamed with everything I had.

I flopped back and soothed my raw throat with the cooling water. I would have to wait. Mary *must* be missing me. When she comes in on a Wednesday, she invariably calls me out for leaving stuff and wet towels around and not making my bed. Today my house would be as pristine as she left it on Monday. That would not sit well with Mary. For sure she would look for me today.

I lay watching the boy play and listening for voices or footsteps above.

Suddenly he dropped his toys and turned to look at me. My heart almost stopped again. I had gotten used to being ignored but now here he was focused on me.

He stepped into the middle of the room and turned his gaze to the hole from where the sun beamed its light, and warmth, and hope.

He stood like that for half a minute as if *listening?*

Then he disappeared along with his toys and furniture faster than an eye-blink.

I lay back and tried to think clearly. Something was happening. None of this had happened before, it confused me. I listened. Nothing but the breeze in the trees, mocking me.

I felt it then, unhidden but welcome. Swelling up from the pit of my stomach, filling my lungs, rushing up my windpipe, through my tortured larynx and out into free air, a scream. A scream so loud and high-pitched It didn't feel like my own voice. I kept it up for a full twenty seconds, pure adrenaline fuelled panic sustaining the effort until I collapsed coughing and choking, my body and head filled with pain at the effort of it.

I slumped back again in the near silence, hope and despair taking their turn, fighting for my soul.

I listened.

The timbre of the sloughing wind changed, ever so slightly. A thin reedy echo-like sound, barely registering on my eardrums, but registering, nonetheless.

I waited breathless. Then it came again. This time the tiny waves of sound had form and meaning, *Briiiiaaan,* they said to me.

I don't remember much of the rescue. The calm voice of the female paramedic, soothing me as her partner worked on my leg. Her gentle brown eyes and toothy smile appeared as the face of an angel. I was surrounded by angels that day.

I remember being hauled up to the surface by an ingenious A-frame made of the firemen's ladders and being carried past the bright red fire truck and the anguished face of beloved Mary to the ambulance.

The next few days I spent in and out of a kind of delirium where I experienced all kinds of painful trials and ordeals. While recovery was bad, physiotherapy was torture. At the end of each day, leg throbbing with the abuse it had received, the nurse would give me the pill, one and one only which would help me drift off to a pleasant place.

* * *

The wonder of the internet! During my convalescence and with very little digging I stumbled upon an old sepia tinted photograph of a small family. A father standing tall in a Confederate officer's uniform, the bonneted mom, stunning in that southern belle kinda way sitting before him in a high-backed wicker chair, and a child.

The child, a boy dressed in a uniform similar to his father's, a cavalry sword across his lap. My heart thumped in my chest. I used that magical method of using my fingers to enlarge the photo and focused on the kids face. I took a deep and shuddering breath, it was him. I had never seen him smile but here he was, happy and safe with the two people he loved the most, his cheeky grin transforming the mournful little face I knew into that of a beautiful cherub. Unusually clear, the picture made it seem that the boy was smiling knowingly at me across the ages.

The photo led me to an 1890 informative article about a southern family named Rafferty that had been devastated by the war.

My young friend's name was Tobias Ethan Rafferty who everyone called Toby. The Rafferty family had bought the house from the builder in 1856 who sold up and went north to avoid the coming war.

Toby's dad Ethan had been successful exporting cotton and importing a myriad of dry goods. He built the tower so he and his wife Elizabeth could sit looking out over the woodlands in the cool of the evening. Ethan copied the plans of a Folly built in Devonshire, England some one hundred years previously. Toby at age 5 had declared the basement of the Folly as his domain and had the servants bring down furniture so he could use it as a playroom.

When war came Major Ethan Rafferty marched north with the 30th Georgia Infantry Regiment. He was killed at the first Battle of Franklin in 1863. That same year, 9-year-old Tobias fell from the top of the Folly and died of his injuries three days later.

A distraught Elizabeth, aching from the loss of both her strong right arm and the light of her life, had the tower demolished and every brick removed from the site. She could only suffer the house for a few more months and then abandoned it to go home to Savannah to be with her family.

The house fell into neglect and disrepair and the Rafferty family were relegated to articles in various Georgia newspapers.

In 1890 the house was bought and refurbished by a New York financier. It then housed 8 families sequentially before being purchased by one Brian Baines.

Elizabeth had her husband's body exhumed and brought to Savannah to be buried along-side his son. Elizabeth joined them in the family mausoleum in 1900 at the age of 70. I plan to visit them and pay my respects when I am able.

* * *

About six months after the events just described, I sat in the kitchen reading the paper and sipping a coffee while Mary bustled about in her comforting and familiar fashion.

"I saw that boy yesterday, Brian, playing around the entrance to the pathway."

My head snapped up! "What boy?" I asked.

"The kid that pointed out the path out to me, the day I found you in the pit."

I had not mentioned the boy to Mary or anyone else. Did she know about the ghost and was joshing me? Mary had returned to her chores at the sink, no sign of guile on her sweet face.

"You didn't tell me about a boy," I said.

"Are you sure," she said, turning and looking quizzically at me. "Oh, OK, maybe in all the excitement I forgot. Anyway, on the day I found you I had been wandering around the lot yelling your name for two hours. Then at one point, just as I was about to give up and go home, I saw a little youngster dressed as a soldier boy standing at the tree line. He pointed to a gap in the trees where I found the path. I turned around to ask him some questions, but he was gone. I decided he must have known something, so I followed the path. The rest you know. I'm sure I told you that."

I thought back to that day and the days following. I was sure I hadn't mentioned the boy, nor did I remember Mary telling me about him either.

Mary stood watching me in her pinafore and bright yellow rubber gloves. I had to say something, even though my mind was buzzing with the implications. I decided to let it pass.

"Maybe you told me Mary and in my condition I forgot. Seems I have a lot to thank the lad for."

"Yes, you do. I'll ask around, he is probably visiting the Banks's in the big house down at the cross-roads, they have little children. I'll tell them what happened and maybe you can buy him an ice-cream for saving your life."

I duly chuckled. "It's the least I can do."

* * *

Many times, I have been back to the site of the Folly. I had had a six-foot high wire mesh fence put around the periphery of the tower floor for safety sake but had made no other changes. I didn't think Toby would like that.

Mary had seen him the day she found me and again that one time. Maybe that was his way to tell us he is still here. I have not seen him again sadly, but I see him often in my dreams. We play and laugh and even tell stories. He is like a son to me in that world.

In this world I like to think that he is still with us. Marching and playing with his toys in some kind of adjacent reality as happy and content as he can be.

Maybe he is on guard. He saved my life once. It gives me comfort to think I have a supernatural protector.

I am not going to hasten my end. I love life too much for that. But as the years pass, I look forward to a time that Toby and me and maybe other people we love can live together in that other world.

Monsters
by Michel Weatherall

There are still times when I wonder where my shovel is. There are times I wonder if I ever owned a shovel. It was on the night of December 5-6th, 19-- that my nightmare began; that I proceeded with my nightmarish obsession.

There are ghouls that lurk beneath our identities, buried. Monsters that live in isolation behind the social masks we wear, unknown of. Sometimes, the rare unfortunate few, see them in our nightmares. I have seen mine. Some monsters are best left buried.

At 9:30 pm my fiancée and I retired for the night. She, being accustomed to an early slumber, subsided to the realms of subconsciousness by 10 pm.

I quietly, very quietly, oh so quietly – why, you'd be awestruck with the silence I exerted! Not a peep did I emit as I inched out of bed. I dressed myself and left our bedroom chamber. As I crossed the hallway to the stairs I walked in close proximity to the walls as the steps squeaked. Oh, what agility I employed! I descended the stairs like a cat, crept through the house in utter darkness, as I was ought to do, its meandering paths and obstacles etched in my memory. I threw on my overcoat, gloves and hood, taking note to bring my father's military issued collapsible shovel. The bus arrived as scheduled, at ten to midnight. My trip requiring only one transfer and deposited me at the corner of St. Laurent Boulevard and McArthur Avenue by 1 am.

The transportation system in the Ottawa-Carleton area is very sufficient and reliable with the exception of terminating at 1 am and commencing at 6 am, thus leaving me stranded in the city of Vanier. In and of itself, not the best proposition in the middle of the night. Being stranded however, at this time, was of no bother as what I had planned to do would occupy the better half of this horrid night.

With the exception of Ottawa's night-shift population, it is amazing the amount of human *refuse* that shambles about in the dark. Night-haunts drifting and riding aimlessly. Drunks, drug-addicts, hookers. Faceless cadavers on a bus.

I see a darkened ghoul across the aisle from me. I wonder how a monster usually reserved to one's imagination can so brash and boldly travel out in the open, until I realize I am staring at the darkened reflection of myself in the bus's window.

I head north down St. Laurent Boulevard to Montréal Road, where I enter the Notré Dame Cemetery, arriving here at approximately 1:30 am. I have always loved the small hours. I am alone. I can walk down the centre of the street – mostly. I own the city. This world is mine.

I had specifically chosen this night due to the frigidness in the air. I had figured that those few stray individuals who visit the dead by night would most definitely be deterred. The night watchman would also be dissuaded from making rounds by Jack Frost, that is even if a watchman were truly there. I could have waited later, for an even colder evening, but I was in fear of *the ground being frozen.*

I walked down a long asphalt path covered over by large tree branches. Although I tried to discern the type of tree, I could not. Trees are alive. The living do not interest me.

Behind the columns of tree trunks lurked illegible tombstones. The icy winter breeze wafts and dances between the tree-trunk pillars of this open-aired cathedral. This is *my* church; *my* refuge. There are only shadows beyond the tombstones. I do not fear the darkness. I know what *lurks* in that darkness. This is my element. I am at home.

After reaching the northern end of the cemetery, the graves became newer and were followed by open sparse black fields. The fields lead nowhere. They feel like the edge of the world. The goal of my hellish obsession lay in a specific plot.

I had a great deal of difficulty in descrying this plot due to the fact that it was an *unmarked grave*. Within half an hour I found the lot. At this point my feet, fingers and ears were numb. I had been out in the cold for nearly an hour. The cold was bothersome and uncomfortable, but it *couldn't stop me*. Spending several more hours *digging* began to look dismal in the frozen climate and being of a sickly frame and possessing a poor constitution dissuaded me further. And as I pondered these dissuasive thoughts my mind strayed...

> *When my mother died I didn't wish to attend her wake. I don't believe attending a wake is respectful, only the contrary. A selfish tradition. It shows respect for the body, not the soul, not for the person! It's insulting. The body is just a piece of machinery. It becomes old. It breaks down. It's disposed of. The soul, the memory of the loved one, is what you keep in fond thoughts. Not the body, not the shell, not the machine. I believe a wake is similar to worshipping a god through an idol. The body – the machine – doesn't deserve respect.*

Many thought of me as being stoic and callous or deeply scarred by my mother's death due to my desire not to attend her wake. Maybe they were right... about the scarring. But there was worse to come.

However, a close friend of mine, an acquaintance I've known for the better part of a decade asked me to attend the wake and when I refused, he asked if not for myself then for him. I did.

I thought on that final moment when they lowered her into the sad slumber of the worm was the last time I'd see her. But something deep inside told me otherwise. I had to see her again. To be sure that I didn't respect and love the machine. I had to see her again and realize that what I saw wasn't her, but only a discarded machine, only a hollow shell where she used to inhabit. I was obsessed.

An especially cold gust of wind brought me out of my melancholic mood. I began to dig. I cannot say with any certainty as to how much time passed as I became absorbed in my fatiguing task. At end, I hit wood with a dull thump. It took me but minutes to completely free the coffin from the earth. I did not hesitate to open the lid, but to my absent mindedness, it was nailed shut. I quickly resolved this with the blade of my shovel. I threw the cover open.

What I saw, I can still see. There is not one night that passes which I cannot recall the terrible sight in minute detail.

The skin, surprisingly, was not dry but looked quite damp, almost sweaty.

The body itself, being exceedingly bloated and gray, on minute study was gelatinous and semi-translucent, or more rightly, semi-opaque. It reminded me of jelly-fruit salad. The one where the fruit seems to magically hover in the jelly. It was the similar case in the body. The bones appeared to be the only real solid structure left and were suspended by the semi-opaque gray gelatinous flesh. I can't be sure what I was seeing was real. Maybe it was my fatigue from digging. Maybe it was the phantasmagoria that the small hours inspire. Possibly my lack of sleep. Maybe it was nothing more than my nightmare; a figment of my imagination.

The face was the most striking feature of the *thing*. The most predominant aspect were the eyes and mouth. In the nighted gloom they appeared as three black dots in the form of a triangle. It was only at close inspection that any detail could be discerned.

The mouth lay wide and agape. Within this abyss rested a swelled black and bloated tongue. The lips... or more correctly, what remained of the lips, were split and severed. A large part of the lower lip hung from the upper, completely separated from its origin and held to the upper lip with thread. The corpse's lips were sewed shut.

The visual organs and eye-lids were completely rotted away, leaving only two wide and somehow staring cavities. The nose, in due time, could have been a fourth hole except for the incomplete dissipation of the fleshly cartilage. Being in a state of partial decay, due to the cold environment I suspect, it had only fallen into the nasal cavity of the skull reserved for the sinuses, giving a caved-in appearance but not an empty one.

It was haunting the way the wind silently made her hair dance. On the odd occasion a clump would dislodge itself and float about.

This was not my mother. This was a rotten, filthy dead machine! My obsession paid off!

I stood, barely keeping my balance in the hole and thought of the first time a child is brought to a graveyard with their parents and are told not to be afraid, for this is a place of rest. If only they knew what horrors slept beneath. The horror which are their and our own futures.

I was satisfied at this point and, replacing the lid of the coffin, scrambled out of the grave, slipping and falling but once. It took less time to close the grave than to open it, so it seemed. The sky was a navy blue when I finished. The sun would rise shortly. I left the Notré Dame Cemetery, crossed the street and headed east to a local restaurant, had a large but unwholesome breakfast then took a ten minute walk to work.

I believe I forgot my father's military collapsible shovel at the cemetery as I no longer have possession of it.

At this point the officials reading my report may question my sanity or honesty. Or capacity. Call it the last vestiges of my humanity. I do not wish to argue nor debate the authenticity of this story. Only to share it. Even to myself I cannot definitely state whether it truly occurred or not. It all possesses an airy, dreamlike quality. Yet what I saw, I still see in shocking detail.

In a way I am glad that this shovel is missing and hope the blasphemous thing is never found. The location of this shovel holds the credentials of this narrative and all it implies. That what I had discovered, the knowledge of what I had unearthed could never be buried. That dark image I saw reflected of myself could never be returned to that shadowy oblivion. That I could no longer deny my morose, macabre, and murderous cravings and intentions for the man who left her in that unmarked grave. In all honesty I do not wish to know the truth. If the shovel remains missing I'll never know for certain. I can continue with the pretension that is my life. If it were to be found in the Notré Dame Cemetery... I pray it'll never be... but not all monsters can remain buried.

Harvest Festival
by Anna Blauveldt

They were lost. Hopelessly lost.

Surrounded on every side by flat grasslands, Adam and Barb were stuck at a crossroads with no signposts and too many options. To the left, distant mist-blanketed hills. Miles away in the opposite direction, a dense wood. Of course, they had no map. Who used maps anymore? And modern technology had deserted them: dead car battery, no cell phone coverage, no GPS.

They might as well have been on Mars.

On the verge of a major meltdown, Barb sat in their vintage powder-blue Austin, fiercely gnawing her left pinky fingernail. She was always, *always* punctual and what was happening now was driving her crazy. This might make them late for check-in at the Rest E-Z Bed & Breakfast. It would *totally* be a disaster if their room were given to somebody else.

Barb was three months pregnant and high maintenance, even in the best of times. That day was no exception, and her fretting finally got to Adam. He climbed out of the car and started pacing back and forth on the dirt shoulder. Surely some friendly motorist would show up soon. Give them a jump-start, point them in the right direction, and they could be on their way. Was that too much to ask?

This fiasco was not the first in their eight months together. But, as creatures of the urban persuasion, they were out of their comfort zone in the countryside. And that made it ten times worse.

Barb had never so much as gone to summer camp as a kid. A recently failed barista trainee, she was fired because she couldn't get the latte foam hearts right. The tall 23-year-old brunette was leaning towards modelling as her next career move. Barb had the looks, but impending motherhood put that plan on hold.

Adam's only childhood experience in the great outdoors had been short and unhappy. After one rainy week in a leaky tent at a boy scout jamboree, he and the scouting movement parted ways forever. Now thirty-something, he was a marginally successful, if cliché-prone, ghost story writer. Everyone told him he looked like Chris Hemsworth in the Thor movies. Only shorter and without the wavy blonde hair. Or the biceps.

Ten more minutes passed. Finally, a vehicle approached from the direction of the forest. They heard it before they saw it. And when it got close, it was so filthy they couldn't tell what make, or even what colour, it was. Just a rusted-out old jalopy, likely held together with spit and duct tape. Its engine made death-rattle sounds when it pulled over and stopped, and they wondered if it would ever start up again.

The driver, when he got out, matched the vehicle. Weather-beaten skin stretched over his spare frame. He had eyes in a permanent squint and a grizzled grey three-day-old beard. It was hard to peg his age. Maybe fifty. Maybe seventy. His clothes were threadbare and patched in places, but at least they looked clean. He greeted them, said his name was Sam, and offered to help.

They weren't sure his dilapidated heap would survive the boost, but Adam pulled cables out of his trunk, hooked up the batteries, and it worked. They were about to drive off when Sam invited them for supper at his cottage nearby. Barb, visibly antsy about getting to the Rest E-Z, was reluctant to accept, but Adam gave her The Look. What's with you? was the message. This man has done us a huge favour and wants our company for an hour. We can give him that. Adam packed a lot into The Look.

They followed Sam into the forest, then turned off the highway and onto a narrow dirt road that eventually led to a clearing. A fast-flowing stream was on the left and a woodpile was on the right, behind a chopping stump with an embedded axe.

In the centre was the cottage. It looked more like a hunting camp than a place to live. Small and boxy, the outside was greyed barn board with asymmetrical windows that seemed to be an afterthought. There was no front step up to the sagging porch; a large flat stone set just above ground level served that purpose instead. The roof shingles, years past their prime, were curled and likely leaked in a rainstorm.

Adam thought the scene looked just like the isolated shack trope he used in his second book.

They parked and Sam took them inside. He told them his wife Molly had almost finished her afternoon nap, and could they kindly whisper till she was awake?

As their eyes adjusted to the darkness, they saw the whole cottage was one large room, with a small area in the back concealed by faded floral-print curtains. Near the front door was a woodstove with a pot simmering on top. Sam said it was rabbit stew. He'd made it fresh that morning and it was almost done.

Opposite the stove was a rough pine table with a gas lamp at its centre and four pressed-back chairs around it. What appeared to be an icebox sat beside another door at the back. Barb wasn't exactly sure it *was* an icebox, but she'd seen something like it on the Antiques Roadshow.

Sam gestured for them to sit. Then he tiptoed to the curtains, pulled one aside and slipped through. Adam and Barb caught a glimpse of an old brass bed covered by a crazy quilt. The curtain closed behind Sam again and they heard him call Molly's name. Minutes later, he emerged carrying his wife in his arms.

Sam settled Molly carefully in a rocking chair facing the stove and adjusted her fringed shawl to cover her better. Then he turned around and introduced them all.

In contrast to the desperate circumstances, Molly had an air of refinement. There was dignity in the way she held her head. Her thick silver hair was smoothed back in a bun, revealing fine lines of sadness around her gentle blue-grey eyes. And even though a shapeless house dress overwhelmed her slight silhouette, it wasn't hard to picture her in an elegant linen frock, sipping tea from a bone china cup and nibbling gracefully on crustless sandwiches.

Soon it was time to eat. Sam moved Molly to a chair at the table and served up his stew. Then the four started to get better acquainted. Barb explained that she and Adam planned to attend the county Harvest Festival that weekend.

Sam smiled when she said this, giving Molly a fond wink. He told them Molly and he had first met at the Harvest Festival decades ago. Exactly how many years he couldn't recall. But things didn't go well for them at first.

The trouble was Molly's parents. She was the only daughter of a well-to-do country lawyer, raised with expectations that she would marry the scion of an equally prominent family in the neighbouring town. It had all been arranged. But when Molly met Sam at the festival, those arrangements fell apart. She was smitten and so was he. To her parents, Sam was simply not suitable. He came from a family of notorious bootleggers. As for his prospects, he'd likely wind up down in the mines. A future for her with him was just not on, as far as they were concerned.

So, of course, Molly and Sam had to elope. For a while, they were happy. And, yes, Sam worked in the mines, but that didn't bother Molly. She was prepared to live a hardscrabble life for him. It was when he started to drink that she found it all too much. She gave him an ultimatum: it was either her or the bottle. After he trashed their home in yet another drunken rage, she moved back in with her parents.

A month later, Sam came knocking – at the service door, of course. He told Molly he was a changed man. He promised her no more drinking. She had her doubts but decided to give him one more chance. And he was true to his word. Sam never touched another drop.

I should be taking notes, Adam thought. This could go in my next book. Or maybe in a short story.

For years, the couple was content in the cozy cottage in the woods. Then one day Molly fell down. And she kept falling down, again and again, as the weeks passed. Something was terribly wrong with her legs. They went to the doctor, but he could do nothing to help. After that, Sam dedicated himself to taking care of her. Now he was starting to falter, too. How much longer could they go on like this?

Their story sounded familiar to Adam. He knew all about genre fiction conventions, and there could only be one ending for Sam and Molly. It wasn't a happy one.

It was time to leave. While Barb thanked the **couple for their hospitality,** Adam discreetly slipped some bills under the gas lamp on the table. Outside, Sam gave them directions to the festival in the next town and waved goodbye as they departed.

It was almost six o'clock when they arrived at the Rest E-Z. They checked in and went straight up to their room.

Even though they retired early, Barb and Adam were late for breakfast the next day. The other guests had already left. On every table, blue cloth napkins were lying askew and white restaurant-stock dishes held remains of meals. Here, bits of scrambled egg and a half-eaten sausage drowned in ketchup. There, a bowl of fruit salad with only the underripe melon balls left. Barb's stomach was having none of that. Instead, she settled for dry toast and English Breakfast tea. Adam dug in to the bacon-and-eggs special.

As they ate, they watched their hosts, Damien and Carrie, clearing the tables. Damien was completely unremarkable except for his eyes. Just like a reptile's, Adam decided. Endlessly darting back and forth as if searching for a juicy bug. And Carrie would stand out in any crowd, floating around the room in a puce caftan, her hair pitch black with a shock of white standing straight up from her widow's peak. The two looked more like caretakers of a run-down off-season hotel than proprietors of a quaint country inn. Barb, already suffering a particularly bad bout of morning sickness, was creeped out by them. But Adam took in every detail, filing their images away in his mind for use in some future manuscript.

Once the couple finished, they joined Adam and Barb. Carrie filled them in on the festival and Damien told them to be sure not to miss the homemade food stalls. Mrs. Bates' famous berry preserves were a must.

Despite their appearance, they seemed to be the ideal B&B hosts: upbeat, helpful, and entertaining. But that changed when Adam and Barb mentioned their supper the previous day with Sam and Molly.

It started when Adam first gave the older couple's names. Carrie and Damien still had their Give-Us-Five-Stars-On-Expedia smiles, but they exchanged puzzled glances. As Barb went on to describe the grim cottage and its dated furnishings, their hosts grew visibly skeptical. 'You can't be serious!' their body language said.

Then Adam recounted what they'd heard about Sam and Molly's difficult life together. Damien raised his hand, palm out, to stop Adam speaking. He, himself, carried on.

"We know all about Sam and Molly," Damien told them. "So does everybody else around here. The two of them shunned because they weren't supposed to be together. Shame how they wound up . . ."

Damien, his left eye on Adam and his right on Barb, explained.

"One Harvest Festival weekend, after Sam hadn't been seen for a while, some of the townspeople went out to their place to check on Molly and him. They found the couple passed away in each other's arms. That was eighty years ago. Since then, their story has become a legend in these parts."

It was Adam and Barb's turn to look suspicious. Carrie added more.

"When the cottage was cleared out later, a hundred dollars was found under the gas lamp on the dining table. The bills looked peculiar, all funny colours, likely made by amateur counterfeiters. There was plenty of phony cash floating around back then. Still, it was surprising that Sam and Molly had anything to do with money like that."

Adam and Barb were dumbfounded. Adam told their hosts the money wasn't counterfeit at all. In fact, he'd placed it under the gas lamp just the day before. It was simply impossible that those bills were discovered there eight decades ago.

They knew then what they had to do, even before going to the Harvest Festival. Returning to their room, they collected their bags, went down to the front desk and checked out. After leaving the Rest E-Z, they took the road out of town and back through the forest.

Ten minutes later, they found the turnoff. The dirt road seemed more overgrown with weeds than the day before, but it was passable. Adam drove on until they reached the spot where the cottage had been the previous day. The stream was there, but it was the only thing that looked familiar. The rest was just a meadow.

The cottage was gone. There was no jalopy, no woodpile, and no chopping stump. Had they stopped in the right place? They decided to park and walk around a bit. Hand in hand, Adam and Barb went over to where the cottage should have been. Even up close, there was no evidence it was ever there.

The couple moved on towards the stream. Pushing through a stand of goldenrod, Adam stumbled and almost fell. With Barb's help, he righted himself and looked down to see what had tripped him. It was a large flat stone. They both recognized it from the day before. It was the step to the cottage porch.

They looked at each other, speechless. This was crazy! How could everything else they'd seen there the previous day vanish overnight? Adam was deeply shaken as they returned to the car and started the drive back to town. And Barb was consumed by only one thought. They had to get to the Harvest Festival before Mrs. Bates' berry preserves sold out.

After parking near the fairground, they rushed through the festival entrance. Once inside, they saw all the amusement rides, games, and souvenir booths any self-respecting third-rate travelling carnival could offer. But they weren't interested in any of that and pushed on.

Adam and Barb passed a family with kids sucking on cotton candy balls bigger than they were. Then came a tattooed couple sporting green buzzcuts and multiple nose rings. A swarm of giggling teenage girls followed, trailing shiny helium balloons behind them.

To Adam, they all resembled stock characters in a fictional midway scene.

The smell of deep-fried something wafted over them as they approached the tent where local produce and homemade goods were on display. Inside, they reached their destination: Mrs. Bates' booth. Carrie and Damien were there, too. They'd just bought the remaining jars of berry preserves. They needed all they could get for their Rest E-Z guests, they explained. Such a shame Adam and Barb showed up late.

For the second time that day, Adam and Barb had no words. When they recovered, they told their hosts what they'd discovered in the forest clearing: the stone that had been in front of the cottage the day before. The smug look on Carrie's and Damien's faces said it all: 'There they go again…those Big City folks are still hallucinating.'

Loot secured and fake smiles restored, they backed away. 'Have A Good Day' was their parting shot. Still cadging those five Expedia stars, Adam observed.

Later, as they drove back home through the countryside, Barb and Adam reflected on their Harvest Festival adventure. The eerie encounter with Sam and Molly. The backstabbing B&B hosts, who would only be getting one star.

And Adam knew he had more than enough material to write his next ghost story.

The Masked Cotillion
by Emma Schuster

A march to the park,
An excuse to be outside.
My worn paperback
Rivals the greens of the trees,
Though its pigment
Is more sickly than lively.

I punctuate pages
By people watching,
Taking fancy to the children
Near the forest's edge,
Whose medieval costumes
Are far too delicate
For a day in the dirt.

Following a surprising maternal instinct,
I take the long way home,
Shadowing the young court
Through the undergrowth.

My brisk step returns,
Hearing belled slippers
Jingle a crescendo.
I can see the jester,
Twirl through the trail,
Joining a freshly seated circle.

My proximity increases
Along with the calls
Of *duck* . . .
      duck . . .
           duck . . .
Goose!

The prancing pink princess
Dashes around her court,
Streamers on her conical crown
Racing behind her, taillike.

The selected soldier
Comes clanking,
But the princess' soft slippers
Betray her,
His metal glove
Enclosing her shoulder.

Pushed down,
Hoop-skirts heaped in mud,
Other helping hands
Grab at her,
But do not pull her up.

Sharp nails make quick work,
Hungry mouths
Bloom erythrocytically red,
Through the messy motions
Of children
And pasta sauce.

Strings of tainted tulle
Adorn the mud.
The stained soldier
Restarts the chant.
Of *duck* . . .
      duck . . .
           duck . . .

Confusing mothering
Manifests for myself,
Turning my back
My stomach turns,
The forest looks sickly -
The green mirroring
The cover of my book.

The ringing in my ears
Sounds like familiar bells,
As my vision arcs skywards
Against my own volition.

Hungry hands help themselves
Ripping like screams from my throat.
I can't help but think
Of the dowdy dresses I used to wear
To play in the same woods.

iWitness
by Matt Lalonde

November 11, 2090 - Remembrance Day
Ottawa, Ontario, Empire of Canada
23:39

Detective Hariette Appleton arrived on scene, at the intersection of Colonel By Drive and Seneca Street in Centertown. She pulled her cruiser up to the Police cordon and displayed her badge to the officer who was guarding it.

"Hey Detective," the officer said as they deactivated the barrier and let her through.

She parked her car on the north curb of Colonel By and was met by another detective. The larger man trundled towards her as she climbed out of the vehicle. His jacket was soaked and his grey hair was matted against his head.

"Bonjour Hariette," he said, almost joyfully, "Hell of a night, eh?"

Detective Appleton pulled the hood of her jacket up, keeping the cold November rain off of her head.

"Sure is Max," she said, "Do we have another one?"

The large man nodded, his double chins jiggling, "Oui. It's just like the others."

"Shit." Hariette said.

She followed the small walking path down to the waterfront of the Rideau Canal where there was a small tent set up. When they walked into the tent, they were met by the crime scene technicians. They all nodded at her and kept working, as she spoke to the senior technician.

"Hello Horatio," she said.

The man stopped and looked at the Detectives. "You will have our findings in an hour," he said with a French-Canadian accent.

Hariette looked at Max, and then back at Horatio. "Okay... but what can you tell me now?"

The technician sighed and hung his head. His ginger-red hair hung in front of his face. "Tabernac," he said. "Okay, we have a dead, caucasian male. Thirty to forty years of age. He was found with his pants around his ankles. His femoral artery looks to have been severed."

"And?" Hariette added.

"And what?" Horatio asked incredulously.

"Was he mutilated like the others?" Max answered.

"Yes. He has the same mark as the others," Horatio answered.

Hariette cursed and turned away. After a moment, she turned back to the redhead. "Send me a picture of the mark as soon as you can," she said, "and thank you, Horatio."

"Ya, ya. Tu nes gentille que quand tu as besoin de quelque chose," Horatio said, waving her off.

The two detectives left the tent and stepped into the rain. Max shivered as Hariette pulled a tin out of her pocket.

"I thought you quit," Max said, almost whining.

She pulled an e-cigarette out of the tin, "Well, stress makes you do things." She tapped the cigarette on the top of the tin, activating it and putting it to her lips.

"That makes Forty-three Max," she said, sucking on the cigarette.

Maxime Raymond nodded, "Yep. In a year."

She exhaled, the smoke forming the cigarette company's logo in the air before disappearing, "And we are no closer to finding the Widow." They were both quiet for a moment before she spoke again. "Head home. We'll meet at the station when we get Horatio's findings." Max nodded, and both detectives headed to their cars.

On her way home, Hariette received a call from a private number. She pushed the button on the steering wheel and answered the call, "Detective Appleton."

"Good...evening detective," came a woman's voice. "My name is Antonia Storck."

"How can I help you Ms. Storck?" the detective asked.

"Actually, I think I can help you," Antonia answered. "You have forty-three unsolved murders on your hands, correct?"

Hariette gave her phone a curious look. "Well, we have forty-two, yes."

"Along with the one tonight," Storck added, "Before you ask, I have friends in the department, that's how I know about tonight's find."

"I see. And how can you help me?" the detective asked.

"I have a piece of experimental equipment that should be able to help you identify the killer. This Widow," Storck said.

"A piece of equipment?" the detective asked, "What kind of equipment?"

"It's a prototype," Antonia said. "Look, I will be landing in Ottawa in two hours. I will meet you at your station at nine tomorrow morning. We can discuss things then. Sleep well Detective," she said, before the line went dead.

Hariette stared at her phone for a moment before calling Maxime. She told him to meet her at the station at eight the next morning, and to bring coffee.

＊＊

November 12, 2090 - Inclusion Day
Ottawa, Ontario, Empire of Canada
08:30

Max walked into the office that he shared with Detective Appleton with a quartet of black coffees from Pequad's. Hariette lifted her head from the desk and looked up.

"Oh, good," she said, sitting up, "You brought the good stuff." She smiled and picked one of the warm cups up.

"Of course," Max said, "It's not like I would get Tim's or anything."

Detective Appleton sat back and drank the black liquid. She pointed at the forty-three file folders. "I pulled them all out," she sat there, "We have a special…consultant coming in today."

Max sat down across from her. "A consultant?" he asked.

Hariette nodded, "Antonia Storck. Apparently she thinks she has something that can help us identify the Widow."

"Really?" Max replied, sipping his own coffee, "That seems…odd."

"Tell me about it," Hariette sighed. "She called me out of the blue last night. She told me she was going to meet me here this morning with the technology."

"When will she be here?" Max asked, taking a bite of a honey cruller.

The other detective looked at her watch. "In about twenty minutes," she answered.

Twenty minutes later, Antonia Storck walked into the office with all the flair of a celebrity. Her designer cloak flowed behind her like a cape. Her dark, angled sunglasses covered her eyes as she stopped at the detective's desk. Her large assistant stopped just behind her.

"Good morning detectives," she said, "Hopefully, today is a good day for all of us."

Hariette stood and held out her hand, "Good morning Miss Storck. Welcome to the precinct. How do you think you can help us?" she asked.

"To the point. I like that." Antonia smiled. She snapped her fingers and her assistant stepped forward with a briefcase. He set it on the desk and then stepped back behind Antonia again. The young woman opened the case and turned it around.

"This," she said, "It is called iWitness." She removed one of the two items from the case and handed it to the detective, "Place one on the head of a recently deceased person, and the other on your head. Through secret, patent pending technology, you will get to relive the last 30 minutes or so of the person's life."

After about an hour of back and forth conversation, Max looked at Hariette, "What's the worst that could happen?" he asked.

"It doesn't work." Detective Appleton said.

Antonia laughed, "It will work. I promise."

Hariette picked up her phone and called her superior. After a heated yet rather short conversation about the ethics of tampering with a body, she had the permission to perform the strange procedure. The two detectives then led Miss Storck down to the morgue. There, they got access to the forty-third victim.

Antonia attached one headset to the corpse and handed the second one to Hariette. The detective looked at her partner, and sat on one of the examination tables before putting the headset on.

"If it turns your brains into an omelet, I get your desk," Max laughed.

Hariette laughed and then looked at Storck, "Let's do this," she said.

Antonia nodded and turned on the corpse's headset. The body jolted and shook for a moment, before once again laying still. Both Max and Hariette jumped.

Storck laughed. "That is expected as the headset is re-engaging the brain. It's normal." She then walked over and turned on Hariette's headset. The detective's eyes rolled back into her head and she fell back onto the examination table with a thud.

Everything was black as Hariette synced with the victim. A moment later, her eyes opened, and she was looking at the trees surrounding the Rideau Canal. She could hear the water running just beyond them, and could smell the wet surroundings. She wanted to look around, but found that she could not move. Slowly, she turned her head, and saw a hooded woman standing beside her. The woman looked at her and smiled. She had a very pale, angular face. Her eyes were red, and dark ringed and her hair was either black or brown – couldn't tell in the night.

The woman looked at Hariette and asked how she felt, and if she wanted another hit. She produced a small pouch that had a soft red glow.

Hariette nodded and replied in a man's voice, saying that a hit would be nice.

The woman opened the packet and poured some of the glowing, red powder onto her thumb. She held it up to Hariette's nose and waited for Hariette to snort it. Once she did, the detective's eyes closed, and then opened again, looking at the dark sky. She heard the woman ask if she was ready for some fun.

She said yes and looked down. The woman was undoing Hariettes belt and pulling the pants down. She smiled at Hariette as she crouched in front of her. A moment later, Hariette was screaming and clutching at her leg. She fell to the ground as blood poured from a slash on her inner thigh.

She was screaming at the woman, calling her all kinds of names and begging for her to help stop the bleeding. The woman stood over Hariette and smiled an inhumanly wide smile. Her teeth had become dagger sharp as she crouched down. Hariette lifted her head, which was swimming with blood loss, and watched as the woman opened her mouth wider than normal and bit down on the wound and a sucking noise followed.

Her head fell back as her vision began to blur. The last thing Hariette saw before blacking out again was the woman standing, wiping blood from her chin and then jumping into the air. A moment later, blackness overtook her and everything went silent.

Her eyes shot open to see Maxime and Antonia standing over her. Max was shaking her shoulders, "Hariette?" he said. "Are you okay?"

The detective nodded, "I'm...I'm good," she said, sitting up.

Antonia helped her up, "You might want to take a moment. Sometimes the use of the machine causes-"

She was cut off by Detective Appleton throwing up into the small sink beside the table.

"That," Antonia finished. She carefully removed the headset from the detective, before walking over to the victim.

"I don't know if I believe what I just saw," Hariette said, looking at the corpse.

Miss Storck walked back over, handing her a small memory stick, "Believe it detective," she said. "It worked. This has everything on it that you just watched."

Max took the memory stick and looked at it before looking back at Antonia. "If we could get another body, one of the previous ones, could we do the same thing?"

Antonia shook her head. "No, unfortunately, the longest time that iWitness can be used is twelve hours. After that, there isn't enough," she paused, searching for the right word, "activity left in the brain."

Hariette nodded and then looked at Max. She told him to take it to the tech lab and get the image of the woman from it. She told him to run it for any matches and get back to her. Maxime left the morgue as quickly as he could, as Hariette looked back at Antonia.

"If this works," the detective said, "we need that tech. Hell, every police service in the world will need that tech."

Storck laughed, "WHEN this tech works, detective, your organization can buy the tech from Storck Technologies. And so can every other agency." The woman began to pack the headsets away, wiping them down before putting them back in the case.

"What...side effects are there?" Hariette asked.

Antonia stopped, and put her dark sunglasses back on before turning back to the detective. "I don't know," she said matter-of-factly. "You are the first person to actually try iWitness." She quickly grabbed the case and then left the morgue.

Hariette tried to follow, but her head was disoriented and her balance was off. She leaned against the table holding the corpse, and looked at it. Her eyes welled up as she looked down at the face of the dead man. Her face.

"No," she whispered, "No, no, no, no, no. I can't be dead. Not ye-" She stopped as she realized what she was saying. After a moment of composing herself, the detective left the morgue for her office. She had seen and heard everything that happened to that man. She was glad she hadn't felt anything, assuming that feeling it would have been horrible.

Hariette was woken up by her desk phone ringing in her ear. She quickly grabbed it and answered groggily. It was the medical examiner and he had told her that the victim, Colton Jones, had died from massive blood loss.

"No shit I died from massive blood loss!" she snapped without thinking.

"Excuse me detective?" the M.E. said incredulously.

"Sorry Mike," she replied, "It's been a strange day. I figured he had died from blood loss. His leg was sliced wide open."

"No detective," the examiner laughed, "There was no blood left in his system at all."

She was stunned. The others had been killed the same way, but nothing had said that they had been completely drained. She thanked the examiner and then hung up the phone as Max trundled into the office.

"I have her," he said, holding up a picture.

Hariette looked at the picture and felt nothing but anger. That was the woman that had killed her. She shook her head. No, that was the woman that killed Colton Jones and forty-two other men.

Max sat at his desk, "Genevieve Devoux. Born in Baie-Saint-Anne in New Brunswick. January first…" Max paused his reading and looked at the other detective.

Hariette raised an eyebrow, "What?" she asked.

He looked at the screen and started clicking on things. "There must be some mistake," he said.

"What is it?" Hariette asked, standing and walking around the desk. She looked at his screen herself. "Born January first, nineteen hundred?" She paused as the information took hold in her mind. That would mean the Widow was almost one hundred years old. That could not be right. Looking at the picture, she would say the woman wasn't a day over thirty.

At the bar on the night of her murder, Hariette had assumed that the woman wasn't older than twenty-five. That's why she had approached her and asked to buy her a drink. She had standards, and wouldn't have gone after a grandmother.

Again, she shook her head, pressing her fingers to her temple and closing her eyes. She had no idea what she was thinking. Memories of the victim kept flashing in her head.

"You okay?" Max asked.

She breathed deeply and nodded. "Regardless of typo's, do we have an address for Miss Devoux?"

Max nodded and showed her.

"Good. Get a team together. I want to bring her in."

An hour later, the officers and detectives arrived at 3080 Richmond Road in the Bayshore area of Ottawa. An ancient house stood there. It had once been deemed a Heritage site, but that had lapsed long ago. Now it was just an old brick house in disrepair. The windows were covered by white, peeling shutters and the roof was in desperate need of new shingles.

The officers carefully approached the house with their weapons drawn. As Hariette's foot touched the deck, the front door opened.

A woman stood in the dark doorway. The Widow. The killer of forty-three men. Hariette seethed with anger as she looked at her killer. Colton's killer. She raised her weapon and aimed at the woman.

"Ottawa Police! Raise your hands and turn around!" she ordered.

The Widow smiled, and then did as she was told. Her eyes flashed red as she turned. Hariette and Max watched as two other officers advanced and cuffed the woman. When they went to bring her out, she resisted.

"My hood," she said loudly, "I have a skin condition. Please, pull my hood up."

The officers looked at Hariette who shook her head and waved for them to bring her out. As soon as the woman was brought out into the sunlight, she started to scream. She started to flail around breaking free from the grip of the officers and fell to the ground. Smoke began to rise from her exposed head as she wailed.

Max ran forward and put his jacket over the woman as the whole area began to smell of burning flesh. Hariette watched in awe as the woman's screams became sobs. Max quickly picked the woman up and took her to the transport van that was on site.

Hariette and the other officers went into the house. The inside was in an equal state of disrepair as the outside. Paint peeled from the walls. Everything was covered in a layer of dust. In the center of the living room was a wooden coffin. It was lined with blankets and pillows and had a hinged top. There was a collection of clothes and glass jars beside the coffin. Of the four jars, three were empty and the fourth had a glowing red powder in it. Similar to the stuff Hariette…no, Colton, had snorted off of the Widow's thumb on the night of his death.

* * *

Back at the precinct, Genevieve Devoux confessed to all of the murders. She confirmed her date of birth, which her ID verified. When Hariette asked how she could be almost one hundred years old, and not look a day over thirty, the woman laughed.

"Clean living," she said, "and staying out of the sun." She curled her lip at the detective as she touched the burn scar that was on her face, "And dark magic," she added.

Hariette asked her about the red powder that was at the house.

"It's a special mix of cocaine and other...unnatural ingredients," Genevieve answered, "It makes people more... pliable." She laughed and sniffed the air. "I can smell him on you detective," she said. "Were you related to Colton?" She sat forward, almost as if she were taking over the interrogation.

Hariette stood, looming over the Widow. "No," she spat. "It is me you murderous..." she stopped herself before she could finish the sentence. Again, it felt like Colton was talking through her.

Genevieve laughed. "What have you done detective?" she asked, licking her lips.

"I have arrested you and am going to put you away for a very long time," Hariette answered.

Genevieve sat back and laughed again. "You won't be able to hold me," she said. "When I am bored, I will simply leave."

"I hope you try," the detective said.

"Better people than you have tried to hold me captive in my lifetime. You're nothing but the next fool in line," the woman hissed.

Hariette stormed out of the interrogation room, and left the rest of the questioning to Max. She sat in her office with a large bottle of whisky, drinking it straight from the bottle.

She kept hearing Colton in her head. Trying to say things. Trying to use her to do something. She took another swig from the bottle and looked at her reflection in her deactivated computer monitor.

"You are not here," she said, "You are dead. This is all just side effects from that damned machine."

She drank herself to sleep at her desk that night.

* * *

March 4, 2091
Ottawa, Ontario, Empire of Canada
16:30

Maxime and Hariette walked out of the courthouse. They both had smiles on their faces as the doors closed behind them. The "Widow," Genevieve Devoux, had been sentenced to forty-three life sentences, one for each victim. She did not ask for any reduction in her sentence. She did not ask for any special treatment. The only thing she asked was that she spend her whole sentence in solitary. The judge was more than happy to grant that request. She was sentenced to the Millhaven Institution in Millhaven, Ontario.

When the doctors examined Genevieve, they could not say why she had such a horrible reaction to the sunlight on her skin, but they agreed that it had to be some kind of allergic reaction. She was allowed to wear a dark hood at all times that she was out of her cell.

"We won that one eh?" Max said smiling.

Hariette nodded, "We sure did." She thought for a moment and then looked at her partner, "I'm going to pay a visit to the Jones'."

"Why? They know what happened," Max asked.

"It's just something I need to do," Hariette answered. Her partner nodded and they went their separate ways.

Hariette arrived at the Jones residence in the West End of Ottawa and stepped out of the car. She smiled as she looked at the house. Her home. It would be good to be back inside. To smell her mom's cooking. See her dad. She leaned against the car and shook her head.

"Not my house," she said to herself, "Not. My. House."

The front door creaked open and Mrs. Jones looked out. "Detective Appleton," she said, stepping out onto the step. "We heard about the sentence. Come in please."

Harictte smiled and walked up the small steps and into the house. Inside, she met with Colton's mother, father and girlfriend. She sat with the family in the living room, smiling for many reasons.

"Did you want a coffee?" Mr. Jones asked

"Sure. That would be great," she answered with a smile.

"How do you take it?" he asked, stepping into the kitchen.

"One milk, one cream, one brown sugar," she answered. She didn't know why she answered that way. She took her coffee black.

"The same as Colton," the man's girlfriend said, choking up.

"Yeah, it's weird but tasty," Hariette tried to cover. She looked around the room, seeing all the pictures of the family. Her gaze landed on a family photo of Colton and his parents.

"That was a good day," Mrs. Jones said smiling.

Hariette nodded, "It was warm. And the ducks. Man they were so loud that day."

Mr. Jones looked at her oddly as he handed her the coffee cup. "You have been to London?" he asked.

Hariette looked up at him. "What? Uh. Yes," she stammered. "It was a long time ago."

The man smiled and sat down across from her. "I'm from London. We were there seeing my relatives," he said, "Colton loved it."

Hariette nodded. "The music scene is so iconic," she said, "It's just…the best."

Colton's girlfriend caught her breath, "He would say the exact same thing," she said as a tear began to run down her face.

Hariette put her coffee on the coffee table and leaned over to the young girl. "Jade, honey, its okay," she pulled the girl into a hug that felt too intimate for the young woman.

"Uh…Detective?" the girl said shakily.

"Shhh, its okay doll, I'm here." She gently kissed the girl on the cheek.

The girl tried to push the detective away, but wasn't strong enough.

"DETECTIVE!" Mr. Jones said, stepping over and grabbing the officer. He pulled her off of the young girl and tossed her onto the couch.

Hariette looked around, wide-eyed. She tried to apologize and explain, but only Colton's words came out of her mouth, pleading for her father to stop this. Pleading with her mother to see that it was Colton. Everyone was either in tears or yelling.

In Hariette's mind, Colton and her argued for control. In the Jones' house, a gun had been drawn. Mr. Jones backed away, raising his hands, and pleading with the police officer to put her gun down.

His pleas were met with a loud bang.

Colton evaporated from Hariette's mind and she was left on the sofa. Her service weapon smoked as a woman screamed. Mr. Jones staggered away from her, covered in blood. He looked down at his shirt and then back at Hariette. Her hand, and the gun fell to the sofa cushion as blackness took over.

Antonia Storck removed the headset and shook her head, "Not enough fail safes." She said. She walked over and removed the other headset from the corpse.

"Okay," she started, addressing the room of scientists. "We need to build more psychic barriers into the transfer circuits." She handed the headsets to a technician, who nodded, "We can't have that much residual bleeding through."

She walked out of the small chamber, and the room went dark around Detective Hariette Appleton's corpse, but she could still see. She watched as Antonia walked through the sterile lab and into a large, ornately decorated hallway. The woman stopped in front of a large mirror, and looked at it. She fixed her lipstick.

"Enjoying the ride, detective?" Storck asked her reflection.

Hariette wanted to look around, but couldn't. She watched as Antonia fixed her hair, and then continued down the hallway.

"Get used to it," Storck said. "You're going to be stuck here for a while."

Hariette tried to scream, but Antonia's will was more powerful than hers. All she could do was witness everything through the other woman's eyes.

The Last House on Macalister Street
by Sara Scally

"And as you can see here the kitchen may be dated but has an excellent view of the yard and lots of natural light. A little paint and you could have a big modern space in no time," the giant fake smile on the real estate agent's face was not hiding the fact that this house was old and in bad shape.

Nancy Wai had been trying to sell the last house on Macalister Street for 5 years with no luck. Even with a booming housing market and a low price, this place was a hard sell. Lucky for her, Mark was broke and desperate.

"Now if you follow me, I'll show you the upstairs," she continued.

Mark's eyes lingered out the window to the spacious yard. It was overgrown and the fence needed work, but it was big enough for a dog to run freely. He always wanted a dog, but Jennifer had been allergic. Following dutifully behind Nancy, he went up a narrow staircase to a restrictive hallway with bad lighting. The rooms upstairs were small with slanted walls and windows that popped out of the roof. It was a little drafty and he could see that he would have to replace them before winter, or his heating bills would be huge. The baseboard heating was going to be the death of him financially, but there would be no help for that for a few years. Not until his divorce was final. If he had any money left to his name, he could have a furnace put in.

"The bathroom is here at the end of the hall and has a beautiful antique tub. The plumbing is more recent than the rest of the house and the water pressure is very good." Nancy was doing her best to find the best features to this old empty house.

Built in the 1930's and not in the best shape, it would be a handy-man's dream, or worst nightmare depending on the money they had to throw at it. Even if it had been in great shape, and in the best neighbourhood, this house would be a hard sell, as it was rumoured that the house was haunted.

"So, Mr. Jones, what do you think?" The long beat of silence spoke volumes. "It may not look like much, but it is in your price range. And you could take possession immediately. It has also been on the market long enough that it's unlikely to draw another bidding war."

There really wasn't much of an option. This was the 9th house Mark had looked at and the only one that he had not viewed with at least one other potential buyer. The housing market had become so crazy that even if a house was in your price range to start with, by the time you were finished competing with other buyers, it was well over. His days of couch surfing were testing the patience of his friends and family, and it was time he had a place of his own.

"Yeah, let's do it. It needs a lot of work, but I need a house," Mark sighed. He needed a home and a place to work, and a place to rebuild. This would do until his divorce was final, the business had recovered, and this global pandemic had ended. By then, he hoped to have this place fixed up a bit and maybe even make a profit.

Nancy couldn't contain her excitement throughout the next couple days of mortgage talks and paperwork. She practically bounced as she handed over the keys and finally ownership papers. You would think this was her first sale. Everyone seemed happy... *well, everyone but Walter.*

* * *

With little to no furniture and a van load of boxes, Mark and his best friend Steven, had everything moved into the house in 2 hours. After the obligatory pizza and beer, Mark was alone in his new home. It was eerily silent.

He walked from room to room planning where to put furniture he didn't have and placing boxes. As the sun set, he lay a sleeping bag out on his air mattress in his new bedroom and tried to sleep. The slow dripping of a tap kept him from peace. Strange, he didn't remember turning on a tap. He had to get a new toothbrush tomorrow and with no dishes or even hand soap and towels, he was yet to use the water in this place. Maybe Steven, who had helped him move, had used the tap in the bathroom?

Getting up, he wandered to the bathroom. Nope. The kitchen. Nope. Where was the sound coming from?

"Great, now I have to call a plumber. So much for newer pipes," he mumbled to himself as he fished his laptop out of its bag and set it up in his lap. A desk would have to be high on his list of must haves. He was in the midst of searching for plumbers when his cell phone started its funeral dirge. Smirking at the ringtone he chose for his ex-wife, Mark answered.

"Hello Jennifer. Find something else you can take from me, did you?" No matter how many times he said he was going to be the bigger person in this divorce, he always defaulted to childish behaviour.

"And lovely to talk to you to, Marcus," the angry voice on the other end snapped. She always called him Marcus when she wanted to talk down to him. His name was just Mark, but by somehow making it longer it sounded like she was being an angry parent. Something about using the whole name to emphasize just how much shit you were in. "My lawyer tells me you bought a house. Without my permission, I might add."

Mark stared dumbfounded at the phone for a solid minute. Unsure how to respond he asked, "Since when did I need your permission to spend my money?"

"You know perfectly well that you are not to spend a single dime of it until after this divorce is settled. I will not have you spending all of it and leaving me with nothing. I gave up 5 years of my life to you, and I'm not just going to stand by and let you ruin my future by spending all that money I helped you make. How dare you think you can spend hundreds of thousands of dollars of my money and not think you have to ask me first." Jennifer's sense of entitlement was no stranger to Mark, but this was a whole new level. The rage in her voice was clear.

"The last time I looked, all of the money you are entitled to you drained from my bank accounts. You have all the money you're getting from me, you blood sucking vampire," Mark shouted into his phone before he threw it across the room. After a moment of silence, he screamed at the top of his lungs until his voice gave out.

It was bad enough that Jennifer had left him for his cousin, but she had taken all the money from their joint accounts, cleared out all their joint investments and kicked him out of his own house. After 5 years of marriage to whom he thought was his best friend and love of his life, Mark had found himself alone and homeless while trying to keep his software business running in a work-from-home age. It was too much. Grabbing the rest of the case of beer from the fridge he sat on the floor and slowly drank himself to sleep.

As the light of dawn crept across the floor and into Mark's eyes, he slowly rejoined the land of the living. His head pounding and throat sore, he found his phone and checked for damage.

Seeing that the money he had invested in a good phone case was still well spent, he noticed the 15 missed calls and messages. All from either the ex or her mother. Deleting them all, he rose to take a shower and start his day. Shuffling down the hallway to the bathroom, he couldn't help but notice that all his kitchen boxes were in the spare bedroom. When he got to the bathroom, he found all his books and laptop in the bathtub.

"How much did I drink last night?" he said out loud. Moving everything back to where it belonged did not take long and after a hot shower, he was ready for coffee and to start his day.

Shopping when everything is closed can be difficult, but luckily IKEA delivers. After a few hours of online shopping to get the furniture he could afford at the moment, he jumped in the car to get food and basics. Hours of standing in line later, he settled into a lawn chair in his living room with a bottle of rum and a case of coke. He had just set up his laptop on a box for some Netflix and booze, when the doorbell rang.

"Who the hell is that?" he said.

Extracting himself from his chair and carefully placing the laptop on the floor, Mark walked slowly to his door. The knocking had become pounding and his heart sank into his stomach as the shrill voice of the dreaded mother-in-law, came piercing through the old wood and glass of his besieged door.

"I know you're in there, you son of a bitch, now open this door before I call the police!" the voice yelled. "How dare you deprive my baby of her future. You open this door right now you hear me? Right now!"

"The neighbours can hear down the street," Mark replied calmly from behind the safety of a curtain. It might be an ancient and yellowed chunk of lace but right now, that lace was the best armor Mark could ask for. "Keep it up and you won't need to call the police, someone else will."

"Open his door you coward!" the woman scolded.

There it was. The one thing Mark couldn't stand. All his life he had held his tongue and been the bigger man. He had walked away from fights and bit back harsh words in school, kept his head down and worked hard. Never took a risk, always checking and double checking before making any move. To some, that made him look afraid and being called a coward was the most insulting thing you could say to him. She knew that and the old bitch used it as a weapon to get what she wanted. Throwing the door open, Mark looked his tormentor dead in the eye.

"What can I do for you, Karen?" the rage was in check for now, but it wouldn't take much to push him over the edge.

"How many times do I have to tell you it's Katherine, not Karen!" the barb was lost on her as she pushed past Mark and barged into his home uninvited, "Now I'm here for the keys to this horrible shack. You have two days to get your crap out of here. My lawyer says that my daughter can claim this place in the divorce as you spent money owed to her."

The righteousness on the face of a 62-year-old, pint sized pit bull, would send the internet into a frenzy. Memes had been made of less.

"I'm sorry, what? Why would your lawyer be involved in this? The last time I looked, Jennifer and I were getting a divorce. My lawyer helped me buy this place so I'm pretty sure it's mine and outside of the divorce so you can't do or say anything about it. Now if you don't mind..." and with a sweep of his arm Mark made a grand gesture towards the still open door. "Get the fuck out of my house before I call the cops."

With the biggest shit eating grin on his face he could muster, Mark waited as Katherine stood mouth flapping like a fish out of water. Not moving, she regained her composure and pulled out her cell phone.

"We shall see about this! I really don't like the attitude you have developed lately. My baby dodged a bullet with you," she said. "Thank god she has a better man now."

Mark's grin fell. The rage was starting to win. The cold look on his face must have scared Katherine because she turned on her heels and stomped out of the house and straight to the car without even looking back. The door slowly closed with a soft thump. For a minute there was total silence, then, with a scream of primal rage, Mark slammed his fist through the drywall beside the door.

Letting the red take over, he punched the front door over and over until the glass shattered.

The spell broken, Mark looked at his bruised and bleeding fist and let the tears flow. The stress of the last few months mixing with the stress of a lifetime came pouring out. Curling up into a little ball on the floor he let it all out while *Walter* watched on in fear.

After what felt like hours on the floor, Mark got up, took a shower and cleaned up his hand. After sweeping up the glass and drywall bits, he boarded up the broken window with packing tape and a pizza box. Sleep came after a bottle of rum.

Walter had seen enough. This man was like all the others, and had to go.

As the sun crept across the floor towards his pounding head, Mark's alarm was blaring. Zoom meeting in 20 minutes.

"Shit! It's Monday! " he yelped.

Reaching out of the cocoon of blankets he had created for his cell phone, Mark realized it wasn't there. Poking his head out he noticed there was nothing in this room.

No, that can't be right, he had a crate he had been using as a night table and a dresser. Sitting up he looked around. The room wasn't empty, everything was on the ceiling.

Frantically untangling himself from the mess of sheets, a very confused and hopelessly still drunk Mark jumped up to get his phone off the ceiling. 40 missed calls and messages. All from Jennifer, Katherine, and some lawyers' offices he had never heard of. Turning off the alarm, he sent a quick reschedule message to his team for tomorrow and looked back up.

"How in the world did that happen?" he asked himself. "I have to stop drinking."

His bladder, finally winning back his attention, Mark wandered to the bathroom down the hall. As he passed the second bedroom the door was wide open and he could see all the boxes marked "Office" were missing. A quick look inside confirmed that they too were on his ceiling.

"Please let the toilet be on the floor!" he sighed.

It was. The bathroom was untouched with one exception. His toothbrush was in the toilet.

After a thorough inspection of the house, Mark called the cavalry. Steven had been his best friend since he was three years old. Through puberty, girlfriends, collage, kids, and now Mark's divorce, they had each other's backs. It took a record 6 minutes and 7 seconds for Steven to make the 25 minute drive to Mark's house.

As they stared at the ceiling and marvelled at how nothing was falling out of the open box of comics they both came to the conclusion that this was not the work of a human being. Three hours of Google searching later, they could come up with three possible courses of action.

One: smudging. The house was clearly haunted by evil spirits and needed to be cleansed.

Two: Feed the Domovoy. Clearly the Slavic house spirit is unhappy and needs to be fed or he will keep messing with your stuff. Research showed that the first owners of the house were Latvian immigrants so they must have brought a domovoy with them.

Three: Burn the house to the ground. Option three seemed a bit extreme so they went with option one then two. After ordering a smudging kit online and waiting for it to be delivered they spilled a bit of vodka in every room in the house.

Satisfied that at least the domovoy would be happy, they spent the next couple of hours taking everything off the ceiling.

Grateful the furniture was still a day or two away from being delivered, Mark thanked Steven for his help and said goodbye to his friend. The smudging kit was coming in tomorrow so he spent his time looking into the history of the house.

First owned by Latvian immigrants in 1938, the house had been owned by 5 people since. An Irish family in the 50's and then in the 70's it had been the scene of a tragedy.

The new owner's son had died when he fell down the stairs. The poor kid was only eight years old. The house was sold soon after but no one had lived in it for long since. Looking around his living room Mark wondered what the place had looked like in the seventies. A quick search of the local newspaper archives had the article online and a photo of the grieving parents in their kitchen. Mark was amused to see the same countertops and cupboards as he had now. The mother looked totally distraught, but the little boy's father seemed cold and unfeeling. It gave Mark the creeps looking at him. It seemed their son Walter had fallen very hard down those stairs. The paper mentioned that he had a lot of bruises and head injuries. A further search of the parents told the real story. Walter Senior had gone to prison a few years later for assaulting his wife. She had been badly beaten and had never regained the sight in her left eye.

"Walter? Is that you?" Mark said to the house at large. Silence greeted him. "I'm sorry for the fighting. I'm kinda going through some stuff right now and I'm not dealing with it very well. My wife left me and took everything. My house, my savings, my dignity, and hell I barely kept my job. Now she won't leave me in peace. Her mother is a relentless, self entitled bitch who won't keep her nose out of anything and now some lawyer I've never heard of is calling. What more can they take from me? I'm tapped out." After a moment of silence, Mark answered himself, "And now I'm talking to myself."

After a longer spell of silence, Mark took himself to bed. Walter had been listening. From his hiding place under the stairs, he had listened as Mark screamed and yelled, he had cowered while the angry stranger attacked the front door. None of his usual tricks had worked to make this intruder run. He had watched as a second intruder came and the two invaders had pondered his existence. It had amused him to listen to their silly theories and he enjoyed being called a house spirit or an alien or whatever a domovoy is. He grew a little concerned when the new trespasser had suggested calling an exorcist. This was his house and they were the ones who did not belong here.

Walter was prepared to burst all the pipes in the house when the screaming home invader called his name. He had not heard his name in so long. He silently listened as the man sounded so sad as he apologized. Walter had never had anyone apologize to him before. Maybe this one wasn't so bad. Maybe he would wait to burst the pipes.

Over the next few days there was peace in the house. Deliveries started to arrive and slowly the place began to look like a home. The smudging kit arrived and other than making the house smell funny, Mark couldn't tell the difference. He had started to talk to Walter as though he was a roommate. Clearly the stress was getting to Mark, but it was 2020 and who wasn't losing their mind being cooped up in their houses 24/7?

Life was starting to settle. As the demand for online shopping skyrocketed, his business increased and he was able to keep his three employees working, albeit from home. His desk arrived and he was able to set up an office. Life wasn't good but it wasn't as bad for a couple of days. Then Jennifer came to end the peace.

It had been a long day with meeting after meeting and Mark had just wanted to reheat some pizza and sit down to finish the documentary on crazy zoo keepers he had started a month ago. It started with his email blowing up, then a call from his lawyer. Jennifer had found a loophole to come after his business. After setting up a zoom meeting for the next day with his divorce lawyer and his business lawyer the phone started ringing.

"Hello Jenifer, what do you want now?" He looked longingly at his, once again, cold slice of pizza. He was never going to get to eat that.

"Mark, we need to talk. I know you have been hiding money from me. My lawyer has informed me that you owe me half of your business."

The condescending voice of the ice queen was a pain to Mark's ears. Where had the woman he loved gone? Not six months ago, he thought he was in a happy marriage. They were making plans for a vacation in the summer and talking about having kids. Now he was alone and the love of his life had become a heartless viper that would only be happy when he was broken at her feet.

"My lawyer will be in contact with your lawyer tomorrow, Jennifer. I really don't want to get into this right now. Have a good night." He ended the call and took the pizza back to the microwave for another round of reheating. He really hoped it wouldn't burn.

A string of text messages made his phone sound like a circus as he watched the plate spin round and round. The soothing hum of the fast cooking appliance blocked out his notification chime. The beep of the microwave almost drowned out as the funeral dirge played over and over. Mark was finally eating this pizza and watching meth addicts play with tigers and he was not dealing with her tonight no matter how many times she called.

He wasn't even half way through an episode when car headlights splashed across the wall behind his head. His heart sank and Mark knew his evening was over. Turning off his laptop he walked to the door before the pounding could begin. He slowly opened it to see an angry ex-wife stomping up his porch stairs.

It would have been one thing to deal with her but hot on her heels was him. Jeremy was Mark's first cousin. He had been a groomsman at their wedding, a friend to both of them, and the end of their marriage.

Cell phone in hand ready to call the police, Mark planted himself in the door frame. "I said my lawyer would call in the morning."

"Mark, this has gone on long enough. Just give me the keys to this place and we will call it even. I'm going to get this house anyway so just do the right thing." Her tone was cold as ice but the burning fire could be seen in her eyes.

"No," he replied.

"Stop being stupid about this," she said. She reached into her purse and pulled out a large envelope with her lawyer's name and address stamped on the front. "It's only a matter of time before I get what I want. Once a judge signs this, I will own this house and your company." The smirk that crossed her face as she waved the papers in his face was vicious.

Taking a step back into his house, Mark was prepared to slam the door in her face when Jeremy stepped out from behind her and right into Mark's face.

"Look mate, you're not going to treat my girl like you did Katherine. You even think of starting anything and I'll send you to the hospital." His puffed up chest and testosterone was evident in his threat.

"Back off and get off my porch before I call the cops. I've had enough of this harassment," Mark said in a calm and collected manner. He was not going to let the rage out this time. No way was he going to let these people get to him like he did last time. The only way he was going to win this fight was to be the bigger man. Besides, Walter didn't like the fighting.

Not taking the higher road, Jeremy pushed Mark back into his home. Suddenly they were kids again and solving their problems with violence. Always bigger than Mark, Jeremy had won every argument by pushing Mark to the ground and sitting on him until he gave up and gave in.

Rocked but not off his feet, Mark prepared for the next move when the plate he had used for his pizza came flying across the room and into the wall beside the door. Stunned, both men looked at the plate stuck in the drywall and then back at each other.

"What the fuck?" Jeremy looked around the room wide eyed. "Who the hell threw that?"

Jennifer, not seeing the plate, walked in behind Jeremy. Not realizing that the tempo of the room had changed, she got right into Marks face. "Stop making this harder on yourself. You should have just given me half of your company when I asked the first time. If I hadn't given you that two grand to start up you wouldn't even have a business. You owe me." She sneered.

"I have paid you that money back twice over already. I have it in writing. As you have been informed, more than once, you are not entitled to my company. A company you have no part of and, until you started sleeping with this asshole, no interest in. I bet you can't even tell me what I do for a living? You already have my investments and savings, hell you even have most of the money I inherited from my grandparents. You have all the blood you are getting out of this stone. Now get the fuck out of my house. My lawyer will be in contact and I never want to see you again. If I do, I will make your life a living hell like you have made mine!" As soon as the threat was out of his mouth Mark wished he could take it back. He had been so careful not to say things like that. Give her no ammo to come after him with.

"Did you hear that Jeremy? He just threatened me," she said. The grin on her face was unmistakable. She had come here to push him that far. That's why she had brought her lover with her; she needed a witness. Turning to leave, the door slammed shut in front of her.

Already spooked by the plate, Jeremy jumped two feet. Confused, Jennifer turned back to Mark. A slow smile crossed his face.

"So, you got what you wanted? You finally got me to say something I can't take back. I guess sending your mother didn't do it. What did you think; using this meathead would trigger a fist fight? Well I'm done fighting with you, honey. I recommend you get out of my house now," Mark said.

All of the dishes in the cupboards started rattling, scaring Jeremy and making Jennifer uneasy.

"I'm not falling for your parlour tricks, Mark," she said. "Let me guess, you've gotten a cat or something. You can't scare me you little shit. I'm not going away. Not until you give me what I want."

"You want this house? Okay. Try and take it." Holding up his keys, Mark made a silent plea to Walter, *"If you're going to do something, now is the time."*

Taking the bait, Jennifer reached out to grab the keys. As her fingers wrapped around the cold metal and fuzzy keychain, all the windows shattered in an ear piercing scream. Lights flicked and the power went out. For a second there was total silence and then the front door started to open and shut on its own. A low moan began as the broken glass on the floor began to rise.

"...Get out..."

Not waiting to be told twice, Jeremy bolted out the door, down the steps and into the car. Jennifer was still in shock. Frozen in place and staring wide eyed at her ex-husband, she dropped the keys from numb fingers. She barely registered the floating glass, or that she had been abandoned. All she could see was the small child staring at her from the stairs. Blood dripped from a huge gash on his head as cold, dead eyes stared at her with malice.

"...*Get out...*"

Moving with impossible speed, the child came for her. Screaming and finally able to move, Jennifer turned and ran as fast as she could. Not even noticing the car, she ran straight down the street. The neighbours, hearing the screams, looked out their windows and a few even poked their heads out their doors, but she just kept running.

"Thank you, Walter."

"*...You're welcome...*"

A month had passed since that night. Jennifer dropped her claims to everything and signed divorce papers. Mark had been able to repair the windows and front door now that his assets were not frozen and he and Walter had settled into a routine and even gotten a puppy. Life wasn't good, but for both, it was better.

Dream Eater
by Summer Breeze

Unsealed windows and doors, small cracks in the foundation, an open vent...you'd think these were the ways they got in. But no, it was the last sigh that left the body before sleep finally claims it that served as a gateway to the Dramora – the Dream Eaters.

They came at night, though they found daydreams equally delicious - the dark was just so much easier when it came to concealing their true appearance. Most humans found their shadowy, blistered, completely hairless forms abhorrent, to say nothing of the cavernous hole that functioned as a mouth, or the lack of any eyes whatsoever.

They had long narrow feet, though they were not used for the most part, not like their arms were. One hand, formed with long digits ending in globular fingertips, held their prey's head immobile and 'read,' or 'projected' thoughts, while the other, a single claw of lethal proportions, served as their only physical means of protection should they be caught unaware while feeding.

But that was a rare occurrence, for they were very skilled at what they did. Their kind had been eating and gathering dreams since the very beginning. They were masters of timing and disguise, with a talent for projecting the illusion of a prey's loved one should he or she suddenly drift into semi-consciousness at an inopportune moment, their minds an intricate network of images pooled from every dream they'd ever tasted.

Rahshen was no exception to any of this, though he did stand out amongst his own kind in another way: he was one of the elite – the rare few who carried so many images within that others actually bowed their heads when in their presence.

Fear and awe were wonderful things.

He streamed into the room and stretched his long body as much as the limited space would allow, opened his senses. He may have no eyes to see, nor any visible ears either, but what he did have was highly-developed. He could pick up the smallest of sounds, inhale the slightest wisps of scent, especially dream scent. Each had its own distinct flavour, with one underlying commonality that defied description. If a human were to try, they would simply call it 'food.'

The family pet growled low in its feline throat, then hissed and shot from the foot of the bed. The slimmest of openings was then put to good use, as it streaked around the bedroom door and out into the hall. The Dream Eater let it go, for animals' dreams were far less tasty than humans' to him, much less imaginative, and focussed instead on the child abandoned to her fate.

The girl slept blissfully on. Rahshen felt it and thought it a shame. Were she to awaken right then, she would shriek in terror and never be the same again for the rest of her days, which would supply him with an endless amount of sustenance for the future in nightmares. Desires of the heart were the ultimate in taste to any Dramoran, but fear was much easier to inspire. He considered provoking her but decided against it; she was already dreaming, and precious night was wasting. Inhaling deeply the scent of her dream – sweet, innocent, and full of childhood delight – he curled his lip. It wasn't much of a meal, and almost identical to another he'd consumed a few nights ago which made it even less desirable, but it would do him.

For a start.

Following the sound of her breathing, he floated upward and came to rest just in front of the warmth emanating from the girl's mouth, his body aligned perfectly just inches above hers. From a small pouch of skin hidden within the folds of his chest he took a tiny piece of himself – a seed of sorts – and dropped it between the youthful plumpness of her parted lips. It would seek out the dream and any emotions associated with it, grow around it all, capture and contain it, before returning to the body from which it came. This left the dreamer with less than what they'd previously owned, but he didn't care – all Dramorans knew that humans could always create more. They'd been doing it since the dawn of their existence.

The child let go of her dream with a small mewl of protest, and within moments the 'seed' was back at her lips, now a blue phosphorescent bubble. He sucked up the ethereal delicacy, tossed his head back and gulped. Down it slid, down, down, down his snake-like throat, until it came to rest gently at his left hip, protruding slightly through one of the many thousands of holes in his skin. Only then, after it had found purchase, could he properly draw on and savour the fresh images and emotions that had entered his being.

In terms of food, they didn't satisfy him for long. A playground, a mother laughing, her arms wide. The girl running, then skipping her way into them, getting picked up and twirled. A few kisses, love and affection, and then the rush and novelty of it all faded, and he allowed them to be contained once more within the bubble, where they would remain unless he required them for an illusion.

The main problem for his kind was that the thrill of experiencing another's dreams was a craving that could never be satisfied; the more they collected, the more they needed to collect. And the greater the emotion they fed on, the greater they wanted the next emotion they fed on to be. It was an endless cycle of need, and like addicts kept from their drug of choice they became ravenous for their next fix. In this particular dream there had been no fear to savour, no underlying veins that led back to a traumatic experience, so....it was time to move on.

Somewhere a dreamer sighed, and Rahshen vanished.

The night went on, from old woman with visions of death, to cancer patient full of anxiety, to teacher terrorized by her students, to soldier missing his family, to pregnant woman worrying over the future of her unborn child. Each of their dreams were tasty to the Dramoran – especially once he'd let his illusions slip and 'projected' his true image into their minds for a second or two - and he was pleased at the diversity, but none of them were the kind he truly enjoyed. Only a heart's desire dream would satisfy him enough now. He knew just where to get one, too, but his dreamer was not co-operating.

Normally the gateway had opened for him by now. He wondered what, exactly, was keeping the man from dreaming? Was he working through the night again? Was he suffering from insomnia? Or had – no, Rahshen *refused* to consider the possibility that another Dramoran had gotten there before him. In reflex he tapped into one of his favourite dreams and drew on the pure fury contained within it, added it to his own. A portal opened and he barrelled his way through it, still seething.

* * *

After a long and tiring night arguing with his ex, all Kevin Parrod wanted to do was fall face first into bed and sleep for a year. Every time he saw her lately they fought, and all he really wanted was to win her back. He was trying his darnedest, but nothing was coming out right. Well, he thought, for tonight he was done. Maybe he could have her in his dreams, or at least get enough rest to get the energy to try again. He thought he must have made it to the bedroom – or at least dozed off somewhere along the way – because the next thing he knew he was looking at the most frighteningly hideous creature he'd ever seen. Covered in glowing blue boils from what he imagined was its chin on down, its elongated body came out of his own mouth (which he found disturbing in itself) and immediately turned toward him.

But that was the least of his worries, Kevin realized, because not only did it have no eyes to speak of while still seeming to stare directly at him, but it was pissed, and at the end of its left arm was a wickedly long claw that could do some serious damage to his person. He thought it a good thing that he was dreaming.

He could have gotten past the enormous mouth - it didn't contain any teeth that he could see – if it weren't for the fact that it was suddenly much too close to his own.

Terrified, Kevin wondered if it was trying to climb back

in. If so, he decided, there was no way he was letting that thing get back in his head, dreaming or not.

He gagged as the fetid stench of the creature's mouth connected with his nostrils. Immediately he shut them down and tried to breathe through his mouth, only to realize that left him vulnerable again. He closed his mouth and went back to using his nostrils, but this caused his eyes to tear up. Blinking furiously to clear them, he was shocked to suddenly find his grandmother leaning over him, touching his face in concern.

Which was really not right, he thought, considering she was dead... and had always hated him.

Which meant he mustn't be dreaming after all. This all felt way too real to him, he thought, to be a dream. There was only one sure way to find out though. He reached out and pinched the back of her hand – hard.

Silently, Kevin swore. He really *wasn't* dreaming. Where grandma had been only a second before, the creature now stood. Floated. Did the thing not even have feet? he wondered crazily. He really needed to focus. And he did, by slamming his fist into the creature's face. Its head snapped back for a second, but then it sort of snarled and grabbed *his* head, pressed its strange fingertips against his cheek and —

Fear gripped Kevin's mind, a terror so strong he didn't think he could bear it. He'd never felt anything like it before in his life. It was unreal. *Unreal.* And then something entered his mouth; in reflex he tried to spit it out, but it had already made it to the back of his throat. He was choking on fear, choking on whatever it was, until it finally left his throat and went God-knew-where but it wasn't down. Kevin heard an unearthly sort of purring, and for some reason that frightened him most of all. Grasping blindly at air – at anything - his fingers connected with a spongy column of delicate bumps. He dug in.

Rahshen cried out as the man's fingers dug into his throat and all the dream bubbles situated there were squeezed beyond what they could withstand. He felt them break open and flood everywhere – inside and out. In a desperate attempt to save them, and himself, he pulled his claw across the man's forearm, leaving behind a long, oozing cut. Then he backed away and gasped in air, covering as much of his throat as he could to hold in what was left of his precious collection. He needed to leave – now – to assess the damage and try to salvage what he could of them. He tapped into the only orb situated deep within him, the one that recalled to him the winds that forever flowed throughout the caves of his home world - and disappeared from view.

Kevin was having trouble believing his eyes. One minute the...*thing* was in front of him, possibly bleeding, and the next it simply vanished. His fingers closed on air and dropped. Yes, it was gone.

Well, he thought to himself, most of it anyway. Some of its 'blood' was still floating before him. In fact, if it wasn't for what he was seeing right then, and the cut on his own arm, he'd be thinking he'd lost his mind. Since he wasn't, he pressed a corner of the bed sheet against the wound and moved on to his next thought: Where did the creature go? And for that matter, why had it been here in the first place? What did it want from him? With no answers immediately forthcoming, and the possibilities alone enough to keep him shaking for the rest of the night and beyond, Kevin made a conscious decision and tucked it all firmly away in his mind. Then slowly, so slowly, his exhaustion overcame him once more, and he fell back into sleep.

***

Rahshen paced from one end of his nest to the other. He was hungry; twenty-three dreams had been destroyed by that human, and he felt their loss keenly. A few of them had even been favourites. He paused to fondle the delicate shells he'd placed in the recovery pod. Gone. All gone. There hadn't been enough left of them to hold onto.

He thought about the other pods around the dark, circular cave – the ones he'd always had the option of filling but had chosen not to. These were not recovery pods, but special cases designed to hold the more unique dreams in his collection. He'd never placed any in them because first and foremost he wanted them with him to tap into at will, and second, he didn't trust any of his race not to steal them while he was away. Those reasons were still valid. Even now, after such a disaster. Also, this would damage his reputation, and he couldn't have that.

Rahshen resumed pacing. If he only had some way to guarantee his return to the same dreamer, perhaps he could retrieve *something* of the lost dreams. Enough for others of his kind to not question him. A previously collected dream from the same person would do it, but he didn't have one, he'd never retrieved the seed he'd planted in this dreamer's head. He hadn't had time before the situation had gone awry.

Then it occurred to him that he did have one thing: the human's blood was still on his claw.

He'd heard tails of one of his kind, long ago, who'd managed repeat visits to a dreamer. She'd found the man's dreams especially tasty, to the point that she'd almost been satisfied. Of course Rahshen didn't believe that to even be possible, but that wasn't what interested him. What interested him was her method of returning to the same dreamer. If he remembered correctly, it had involved nicking the human right before she departed each time, then, when the next portal opened, sticking her claw through it first. It supposedly acted like another kind of homing beacon. The DNA in the blood recognized and sought out its match in time and space.

Or so the story went. He was about to find out if it was true.

* * *

Kevin was dreaming. Oh, how he dreamed! Like he'd never dreamed before. There were people he'd never met before but felt safe with, and places he'd never been yet pictured with such clarity. It was really quite bizarre, especially when he looked down at himself and felt a baby kick within his own womb. He knew it was wrong – so wrong – but couldn't help feeling protective regardless. And worried. He smoothed his hand over his rounded stomach in reflex. It flattened, and suddenly he was in a hospital bed with tubes sticking out of his arms. Fear struck him then – the fear of death.

There is something worse than death in here.

Like what? he wondered. He had a feeling he should know, but the answer was eluding him. He turned his head and looked down a long green corridor. Maybe it was down there.

Rahshen smelled it the second he hit the room. Dream-scent. And this one was very strong. His mouth opened wide in anticipation: soon it would be his. He float-crawled his way to where the dreamer lay, rested his fingers lightly on the man's cheek, 'read' him. And that's when he knew he'd made it back to the same one as before. This, he thought, was going to be the best meal he'd ever had. He'd make sure of it.

But wait. What was this? A heart's desire hidden from the dreamer himself? Not only hidden, but not even sought. Instead, the man sought....

Oh.

He mind-stared at the tucked-away image of himself in the firm grip of rage right above his prey. Is that how he appeared? Rahshen thought absently. He'd projected his image many times, but never had he imagined how a human mind might perceive it. It was quite different. Mentally, he shook his head and pushed the image aside. It wasn't important right now – interesting, but not important. He would just distract the man, who had obviously decided their encounter was too traumatizing to look at anyway, maybe use the image with another dreamer sometime. What *was* important right now was the fact that here was what he'd been looking for, swirling amongst the remnants of all the dreams he'd lost. The man must have inhaled them. If the seed he'd left here could contain all of this, he may be the first of his kind to *fully* satisfy his craving for collecting.

At least for a moment.

But what a moment it would be! He focused all of his attention on redirecting the man's current stream of thought.

Kevin reached the end of the hall and found himself face to face with a room full of extremely hyper school children. Frustrated at the delay, and more than a little shocked at the sudden and rapid firing of enthusiastic questions in his general direction, he plowed across the classroom as quickly as humanly possible. Unfortunately, the mob of youngsters followed him - all but one, that is - clinging to his legs like psychotic little monkeys. Something about the lone child made him want to pause, but the faces of those in front of him quickly changed to suit their actions - with shrieking mouths demanding to be heard, until he thought he would go crazy at the noise - and he had to go. He covered his ears, struggled to shake them off, and plunged through another door. Had he wanted children? he thought wildly. Maybe he'd rethink that one.

No no no! Frustration pooled inside of Rahshen; children should have led the man *to* his ex-wife, not *away* from them; they were supposed to be linked to the human's desire for her, but it had all gone wrong. The dream wouldn't even form at this rate.

He checked on the progress of the seed, and found it to be growing fine but in too large a shell to be retrieved in the usual way. That would still be all right, thought Rahshen, except that it would ruin the man's mind for future dreaming. He realized he would have to separate the man's thoughts or lose everything. It would still be a large meal, just divided into smaller portions. A bit disappointing, but still salvageable. Twenty should do it in his estimation. Not quite the number he'd lost, but not everything was here. He dropped the seeds into the man's mouth and got to work.

Deep within his mind, Kevin turned his head. Something was happening. The comforting arms of his mother surrounded him, kept him safe, but like any child his curiosity was too great.

Or was it his mother? he wondered. He looked up at her again and saw his wife, Jennine, instead. Yes, his wife, he thought, not his mother. His wife... He felt joy begin to spread throughout his chest. Here was his chance to win her back.

Suddenly, off to his left, a death's head appeared in a tree. Kevin opened his mouth and screamed like the old woman he was, then quickly curled his frail body into a protective ball around Jennine.

In the next second everything was gone. He wondered why he was curled up, and stretched, looked up at his mother and smiled. Her face morphed into a grey thing with no eyes, a thing that had the biggest mouth and –

It disappeared.

Above him, Rahshen cursed. The man was starting to recall details about what he'd seen, and to make matters worse, this latest bubble had removed his projected image of the man's ex-wife. With everything swirling around in there, it was bound to happen; he couldn't possibly separate everything fast enough. Good thing, Rahshen thought, that the dreamer had lost this particular memory, and that Dream Eaters could project any image they desired. He quickly checked the details of what he required and re-entered the dream stream.

Kevin, meanwhile, was wondering where he was and what he'd been looking at. He couldn't remember what he'd been about to do. And where had all these children come from again? he thought. They were horrible, just horrible, but Jennine was here so she would take care of them. She would calm the little monsters if they didn't eat her alive first. He should help her, he realized, and he would if it weren't for all the tubes all over him, and that his family needed him, and –

The thoughts vanished as though they'd never been and Kevin felt tired, so tired, but didn't remember doing anything particularly exhaustive. A vague sense of unease rolled through him. It didn't make sense that he was so tired, yet he felt like he had when he'd studied for exams in university - as though his mind had been working overtime. He looked down the long, narrow hallway to the door and determination grew within him. Something was behind it, he was sure of it. It felt huge whatever it was, and terrifying, but if he wanted an answer he'd have to seek it out and face it. He began walking again.

Again? Had he been walking? Kevin asked himself. He thought he might have been. Yes, he had, he silently replied, before the... the... well *something* must have stopped him the first time. It struck him as odd that he couldn't recall what it had been - that he couldn't recall much at all. Maybe opening the door would explain that too. He picked up his pace.

A small boy appeared in the hallway to his left. Kevin stopped short in surprise, then watched the child pull something out of his pocket and get down on his haunches. Carefully and precisely, the boy placed stones of different shapes and lengths on the floor, then looked up at him and smiled. Intrigued, yet not wanting to get sidetracked from the door, Kevin merely nodded in response. The child looked sad then, but Kevin steeled his heart and walked on.

Rahshen grunted at this surprising turn of events, then furiously got to work inserting the image of the man's ex-wife wherever possible; it consistently produced the strongest emotion in his prey and distracted him from the door. But the dreamer was constantly being pulled away from 'her' by the remaining lost dream images, so he also kept a mental eye on the progress of the rest of the dream bubbles. As soon as each reached a critical size, he 'called' it back to himself and inhaled it. Eating them one after another was giving him the biggest rush of his existence. So close, he was...so close... Soon, he thought, he would be tasting the best one of all.

She was everywhere Kevin turned. Maybe, he thought, it was a sign that all was not over between them. They really could work it out. Things were certainly going well. They were at the cabin now, a place they both loved, and they weren't arguing. He handed Jennine a drink and used the opportunity to enfold her in his arms from behind, look out at the night sky with her. It was full of stars and absolutely gorgeous, but not as gorgeous as the look in her eyes when she lifted her mouth to his; it was all he'd ever dreamed of seeing there again. He claimed her lips gently, then looked back out at the water with a deep, contented sigh.

They didn't talk much, but there didn't seem to be any need to. Instead, they stood on the grass as they were, and watched the sky rapidly lighten. To Kevin's surprise the boy from the hallway appeared on the bank before them. Like before, the child pulled stones from his pocket, got down on his haunches, and started arranging them. Kevin watched him for a moment, strangely drawn, but unwilling to leave Jennine. Slowly, as if sensing his indecision, she pulled his arms from around her and stepped away.

Outside of the dream, Rahshen quivered in anticipation. Finally, after all his hard work, the human was right where he wanted him. He gave him a little push to speed things up, and waited.

Kevin stared at Jennine, then at the boy, then back at her. She was encouraging him to move if her small shove was anything to go by. Then she made *shooing* motions at him, leaving no doubt in his mind. He went to the boy.

"What are you making?" he asked him. It was long and narrow, whatever it was, and so familiar. The boy didn't reply, but kept on with his creation. Rocks in the sand that were slowly but surely forming a shape Kevin knew. An airplane. It was an airplane. Just like the ones he'd made as a child.

In the sand. With rocks.

He used to love doing that. In fact, he'd sort of imagined way back then that he'd grow up and build real ones. Life had intruded of course, and taken it from his mind. And then he'd met Jennine, fallen in love, and the last of it had gotten lost in trying to make her happy. For what? he thought wryly. She'd left him anyway.

Kevin took a good look at the boy beside him, his mind so much clearer now, and knew he was looking at himself. He turned to Jennine to tell her what he'd discovered and found her hanging over him. He rose at the look on her face.

"And now you are mine." Her demeanour was smug, so smug, and her voice.... it was not her usual voice. She spoke in a sort of purr - low-pitched. In dawning horror Kevin realized where he'd heard it before. The door in his mind flung wide open then, and he felt sick with fear. As if in accord, the sky around him began to swirl alarmingly. Giant, smokey tendrils formed out of nowhere and began to encompass the cabin, the lake, *them*. He saw a way out and turned to run.

"Oh no, you don't," the Jennine who was not really Jennine at all growled, clamping down on his shoulder with amazing strength. "I want you to see your dream disappear, feel it. You deserve it after what you did to me, what you stole."

Kevin struggled to untangle his shirt from the creature's claw as it floated them up into the sky. It had dropped all pretense now and was in its true form. "Stole?" he said. "What do you mean, 'stole'? I didn't steal anything. You attacked me in my bed and I defended myself! So you bled a little. I bled too. Let's call it even. You can let me go, leave and never come back. I won't say anything to anyone about your existence. I don't even know what you are for God's sake!"

Rahshen shook him. "Oh no, we are *not* even. You owe me a meal!"

"A meal?" Kevin cried, bewildered and terrified, all at once. He was trying desperately not to turn around and cling to the thing at this height. "What are you talking about!"

"I am a *Dream Eater*," Rahshen roared, "a *collector of dreams*, and you have destroyed part of my collection!"

All the pieces fell into place. The blue orbs he'd destroyed, they hadn't been blood at all, but dreams. Kevin looked at the sky. And this was one of them, come to take his dream away. He looked down at the small figure below. He would be eaten along with it. Would he feel it? Would Kevin, the grown man, remember any of it if his child self were consumed? Not likely, he realized, and he'd only just discovered how much it all meant to him so he wasn't really willing to let it all go just yet.

Which meant there was only one thing he could do now: fight. And if this was all a dream...

Kevin imagined his shirt gone, and suddenly he was free-falling through the sky. It was a terrifying feeling, but accomplished in seconds what he'd hoped for. He gasped in air and sat up in his bed, wide awake. Above him, the Dream Eater roared.

"You think you have won?" it demanded in a low, sinister voice a moment later."You have won *nothing*. Eventually you will fall asleep, and I," - it leaned in so close Kevin choked at the stench of its breath - "will be here when you do."

And it vanished.

The Forgotten Dress
by Jana Begovic

Her hand trembled when she raised the white porcelain cup to her lips for a sip of coffee. Gazing through the coffee shop window, she watched the patio fill quickly with people on this splendid sun-drenched day. However, she wanted to sit inside in a secluded corner and try to gather her thoughts in solitude.

Her marriage was quickly unraveling at its seams and no amount of effort could stitch it back up. Their clashes were more and more frequent, deepening the chasms of divide between them. All of a sudden, he began pressuring her to leave her job as an editor in a publishing house, arguing that as a software developer, he was making more than enough money to meet their needs. She could not explain to him that it was not a matter of money; her job was her passion that was closely tied to her educational background in postmodern literature and her deep love of reading. He wanted her to conceive, to have children and devote her time to raising them, as most women in the culture he came from had done for centuries.

Furious with him, she would tell him to go back to his homeland as she had little in common with the culture of his birth. She had not gone to graduate school to be held in the captivity of domestic life. Moreover, she did not intend to change the way she dressed in order to reflect whatever standards of feminine elegance the women in his country of birth embraced. She resented being compared to his sisters and some elusive but high standard she was unlikely to reach.

Replaying their latest fight in her mind over her getting a Pixie hair cut without having consulted him, she forgot she was holding a cup of hot coffee in her hand, and she stifled a scream of pain when a splash of the hot liquid fell on her bare knee.

Quickly, she placed a napkin on the affected skin absorbing some of the coffee and looked around in search of more napkins so that she could mop it off the floor, when a male hand proffered a wad of them. She raised her eyes and locked gazes with a man who looked about fifty years old, and whose green eyes seemed to sparkle with amusement.

"Did you burn yourself?" he asked, and she detected an undertone of concern in his melodious voice.

"Not really," she replied and looked at her knee that was slightly red. "And thank you for the napkins."

A smile frolicked on his lips when he said, "I believe I know you from a book reading. In fact, we have a friend in common. I went to Alan White's book launch and it was you who gave an introductory talk about his book for which you had also written a foreword. Is my memory serving me right?"

He looked at her with expectation in his eyes. At the same moment, a barista called, "Damian," and the man excused himself and went to get his coffee.

She remembered that she had not been able to stay long at Alan's book launch, as she had promised her husband she would be back home in two hours at the most. Anger swelled up within her thinking about her husband's possessiveness and jealousy making her feel enslaved in her marriage.

"May I join you? I have about half an hour before my next class starts," asked Damian holding a cup of cappuccino in his left hand.

"Yes, of course," she said extending her hand. "I'm Eliza. And yes, I was the one who had introduced Alan's book that night. He is a close friend. His book was a great success. I am normally not drawn to the supernatural in literature, but the ghosts in his story were so credible.

"So, I suppose you teach across the street at the school of comparative literary studies, right?" asked Eliza.

"Excellent guess. I teach graduate courses," he replied.

"I did my Ph.D. there and soon after graduation I got a job as an editor at the Neptune Publishing House two streets down," said Eliza.

They spent the next 30 minutes in animated banter about arts and their influence on each other. They also talked about the manuscripts she was currently reading and considering for acceptance for publication. Damien mentioned he was working on a book of non-fiction about the political influences of postmodern writers, and once his manuscript has been completed, he would like to submit it to her publishing company.

When he stood up to leave, he said he hoped to see her again.

"I usually spend my Wednesday lunch hour here," blurted Eliza feeling a blush tint her face because of the lie she had just uttered.

"It's a date then," Damian said winking at her.

She was stunned by her not so implicit invitation that they meet next Wednesday. She also realized how much she had yearned for conversations linked to literary theory and arts, in general. That she felt attracted to Damian, she would not dare admit to herself under any type of coercion.

Once she arrived home, she looked at her phone and saw that she had missed four calls from her husband. She called him back and lied that she did not hear the phone ring as she was engrossed in editing a manuscript and the phone was in her bag.

The following Wednesday, Eliza put on a pair of newly purchased white designer jeans and a lavender form-fitting shirt. She wanted to look casual-chic.

Entering the coffee shop, she could feel a frenzied swirl of butterflies in her belly. "What in the world is happening to me?" she thought, considering leaving while there was still time.

The door opened and he came in looking rushed. His grin was wide and warm upon seeing her.

"I hope your lunch break can be extended as I'm free this afternoon," he said animatedly.

"Sorry, I can only stay an hour as we have a meeting I could not possibly miss," Eliza replied pleased she did not have to lie about her afternoon commitments.

Again, minutes flew by on the wings of star-filled gazes and captivating conversation about arts and literature, as well as the current political happenings. In one of his passing remarks, he mentioned that his late wife had owned a bookstore.

"How long ago did she die?" asked Eliza.

"It will be four years at the end of this month."

"What did she die of, if you do not mind my asking?"

"Suicide."

A shadow passed over Damian's face and Eliza steered their conversation in another direction.

When she looked at the time on her cell phone, she stood up saying she had to leave in order not to be late for her meeting.

"See you next Wednesday, then!" Damian exclaimed and she nodded.

Wednesdays at noon became their regular meeting time. The attraction between them was palpable and Eliza felt she was cheating on her husband, as Damian had become part of her day and night dreams. She felt she was walking on clouds, intoxicated with the feelings of infatuation.

When after one meeting at the coffee shop Damian asked her out to dinner, she decided it was time to break the spell and tell him she was married and would not meet him for dinner until her divorce was finalized. She asked him for his phone number saying she would contact him once she was single again. Wordlessly, he wrote down his phone number, his email address as well as his home address on a piece of paper he pulled out of his knap sack, and handed it to her.

That evening, she packed whatever could fit in a large suitcase and left her apartment. She sent her husband an email in which she explained how she had felt unhappy in their marriage for a long time, how incompatible they were and how she wished he would find the right kind of woman for himself. She also said she did not want anything from him but an uncomplicated divorce.

Eliza's mother lived about an hour away from the city centre where Eliza resided, and she welcomed her daughter with arms wide open. She only said Eliza was lucky not to have had children, because moving on would have been more complicated.

It took only three months for the divorce papers to be finalized, as unexpectedly her husband had readily agreed to all the terms proposed by Eliza's lawyer. Eliza realized that he had also probably been unhappy with her and welcomed the chance to start a new life.

She celebrated her divorce with a small group of friends in a cozy restaurant and after a couple of glasses of sparkling wine, mustered up courage to send Damian a text message proposing they meet at the coffee shop the following Wednesday. His response was almost immediate and radiated with joy. He said that hearing from her was one of the most thrilling surprises of his life.

Their relationship developed at a dizzying speed. Eliza had never felt so madly in love before. When he proposed to her during a walk through a meadow full of wild flowers, she was so choked up that she could only nod her head in silent acceptance.

After their honeymoon in Italy, they moved into Damian's charming redbrick, Victorian house and began renovating it. As Eliza's grandmother had left her a small inheritance, Eliza decided to invest it into turning Damian's house into a more contemporary space. His ex-wife had furnished it with heavy and old-fashioned pieces of furniture, burgundy curtains and had painted the walls in dark grey. The hardwood floors were of a reddish hue. Eliza liked airy and light spaces, as well as white walls and blonde or walnut hardwood floor and furniture. Damien told her to redecorate and renovate the house according to her taste, as he had been reluctant to make any changes after his first wife's death, but was finally ready for a new beginning. He had purchased the house before he was married to Fiona, but had let her furnish it the way that made her happy.

Between her job and meetings with the contractors, Eliza found herself busy, but also filled with enthusiasm and content with the changes rapidly taking place in her new home. The living room was suddenly converted from a gloomy and oppressive space into a light and bright room with large French doors opening onto an expansive garden.

One evening, after cleaning the dust and splotches of wall paint on the new hardwood floors left by the contractors, Eliza went into the bathroom to take a shower. Just as she began taking off her makeup, she screamed and froze having seen the reflection of a woman in the mirror above the sink. The woman in the mirror had long brown hair and her eyes were wide open as if in wild disbelief or anger over seeing Eliza. She wore a bright red satin evening gown with a sequined silver piping along the deep plunging V-neckline. When Eliza turned around, the woman was gone. Shivering in fear and panic, she ran back into the living room looking for her cell phone. She called the police saying there was an intruder in her house. She also called Damian who left his class in the middle of a lecture to rush back home.

The police arrived after a few minutes and searched the house thoroughly, as well as the back and front yard finding no sign of an intruder. All the doors and windows had been closed, and there was no evidence of an attempted break-in. They asked her to describe the woman and as Eliza began describing her, she noticed the pallor in Damian's face.

After the police had left, Damian poured her a glass of cognac and she drank it even though she disliked hard liquor.

The next few days she ensured she was never alone at home. She went back to work and scheduled contractors in the afternoon hours.

One day, while sitting in the living room and admiring the new elegance of a light coloured hardwood floor and white sofas with blue cushions, she heard the sound of glass breakage coming from upstairs. She had thought one of the workers, who was painting the bedroom and hallway walls, had broken something, and she ran upstairs to check. When she entered her and Damian's bedroom, she found the glass frame of their wedding photo smashed beneath the dresser it had stood on. She picked up the shards wondering how the photo could have fallen off the middle of the dresser. She also felt a sudden chill in the air as if the room had suddenly become cold in spite of the warm September weather.

When she turned the doorknob to go back downstairs, she could not open it no matter how hard she twisted it and pulled on it. At the same time, she felt an icy breath on her neck and froze in fear not daring to turn around. Her mouth went dry and her heart palpitations became so intense that she thought she would die of sudden heart failure. When the door opened, she collapsed in the arms of one of the workers.

"Are you alright, ma'am? I could hear you trying to open the door as I was passing by. We are done painting for the day."

"Thank you, Sam. I guess the knob got stuck, somehow." Eliza composed herself, and moved quickly past Sam and called Damian as soon as she found her phone. Her voice faltered as she was trying to explain to her husband what had happened. She told him she was sure the woman she had seen in the bathroom was still in the house.

Damian tried to calm her down and told her that the bedroom doorknob would sometimes get jammed and that it needed to be changed. He suggested they go out for dinner and she agreed.

When they returned home, Eliza went straight to bed feeling emotionally and physically exhausted. She fell into a deep sleep dreaming about running through a dark alley and trying to escape from something evil that was pursuing her. Just as she was about to turn a corner and step into a lighted square, someone grabbed her by the neck and started strangling her from behind. She screamed and trued to pry off hands with blood-red nails. She woke up screaming and gasping for air. Damian was trying to embrace her but she was too hysterical to allow him to touch her.

"There is something evil in this house and it is trying to harm me," she sobbed. "I am not crazy. I am not imagining things. My neck hurts."

"It was just a nightmare, honey," Damian said in a voice brimming with worry upon seeing red marks on Eliza's neck.

Eliza suddenly turned toward him and said, "Show me a picture of your wife and tell me how she died and what had happened between you."

Damian looked uncomfortable. "Can we leave that conversation for tomorrow, it is 2 am."

"No," exclaimed Eliza. "I want to know everything about her. I have a feeling her ghost is haunting this house and cannot tolerate my presence."

"You believe in ghosts?" asked Damian incredulously.

"How else could you explain the woman I saw in the bathroom mirror? There were no signs of break-in."

"What do you want to know?"

"Why did she kill herself?"

Damian sighed and said, "I was going to leave her. Fiona was mentally unstable, but would not seek help. She would get into fits of rage and throw things at me. This little scar on my forehead was the result of a cut with a porcelain cup she broke on my forehead. When I said one day I'd had enough and was leaving her, she threatened she would kill herself. I didn't believe her, but to my horror, I found her dead one day on the living room sofa. She had taken a full bottle of sleeping pills."

"So, she died in this house?"

"Yes," Damian replied softly.

"Did she have a red satin evening gown?" asked Eliza pacing the room.

"I believe she had a red gown that she wore once for the official opening celebration of her bookstore. I remember thinking she looked a bit overdressed for the occasion."

"Where is that dress?" asked Eliza excitedly.

"I'm not sure. I gave away most of her clothes and possessions, but there may still be some of her belongings in the attic. She kept things there she no longer wore and planned to discard," said Damian.

They were both wide-awake now, while outside, the night had already begun to recede before the dawn.

"I want to search the attic now," said Eliza decidedly.

"Put your shoes on as there may be broken glass or scattered screws and nails on the floor," said Damian.

When Damian turned on the light in the attic, Eliza saw a couple of old velvety armchairs, a bookcase that had no books on the shelves, but only a bookend in the shape of a bear made of green stone that looked like malachite. In the right corner, below an oval window was a large blue plastic box.

"What's in the blue box?" she asked.

"Fiona's stuff, I believe. It seems I had completely forgotten about it; otherwise, I would have gotten rid of it."

When Eliza opened the box, she found woolen skirts and sweaters in the first couple of layers.

"She kept the winter clothes she no longer planned to wear in that box," said Damian.

Eliza placed the clothes on the floor beside the box and continued rummaging in it. When her hand touched a silky fabric, she pulled it out from under a black sweater and spread it on the floor. Before her eyes lay the red satin dress she had seen on the woman in the bathroom. The dress looked brand new.

Eliza cast one last glance into the box and saw a small photo album on the bottom. She opened it and let out a gasp when a photo fell out of it. In it, a woman with long brown curly hair, wearing the red satin dress was standing in front of a large bookshelf and holding a glass of champagne. On the back of the photo was the inscription, "Bookstore opening night."

The pallor in Eliza's face and her trembling hands alarmed Damian.

"You look like you'll faint. Let's go back down," he suggested.

"No. We need to do something about this dress. I know what. We must burn it. Remember Alan's book launch? In the passage he read that evening, there was mention of burning a sweater that had belonged to the ghost haunting a Mediterranean villa. That is how they got rid of it. Do you remember that Alan had said his book was inspired by a true story? Maybe, the dress is her last connection to this house. Maybe the haunting will stop if we destroy it."

Eliza left the attic and went into the kitchen. She took from a cupboard the large metal bowl she used for salad preparation, and then searched for matches. She also remembered the cigarette lighter she put in a kitchen drawer after she had found it in the backyard. She had assumed one of the contractors had forgotten it there. The last thing she grabbed was a pair of scissors before she went back to the attic.

Damian held the dress while she cut it into small pieces. As she was cutting it, they could hear the banging of doors downstairs and the rattling of windowpanes.

Damian smashed the cigarette lighter with the bookend and let the lighter fluid drip on the dress pieces. He then lit a match and dropped it into the metal bowl. The pieces of satin began to burn slowly making a spluttering noise. Suddenly and out of nowhere a chilly wind rose in the attic and crackling noises could be heard from all corners along with the sounds of moaning alternating with hissing.

"She's here," whispered Eliza and threw more lit matches into the bowl. In the smoke rising from the burning dress, they could delineate a contour of a face contorted into hideous grimace of madness, howling in rage and denial.

When Eliza spotted a yellowed newspaper protruding from under the bookcase, she quickly pulled it out and threw into the fire to feed the flames, even though she feared the flying sparks might fall outside the bowl, and start a fire that would engulf the entire house.

Screams echoed as the dress turned into black ashes. The floor of the attic trembled and Eliza thought the house would splinter in half.

When the last piece of the dress burned down, the tremors in the floor ceased, and an eerie quiet descended on the house. Damian offered Eliza his hand and helped her get off the floor.

The sun was shining outside and they could hear birds chirping.

"Could it be that we have gotten rid of her ghost?" wondered Eliza aloud.

"Let's sell the house and start anew, unencumbered by my past," said Damian, visibly shakened.

"I'm no longer afraid of her ghost," replied Eliza, " but I would like a brand new house, uncontaminated with the energy of other people. Looking for one, or having one built could be an exciting project."

"New beginnings are invigorating. Let's raise a glass of bubbly to that, even if it's only 9 am," said Damian.

Eliza nodded smilingly.

Framed
by Codi Jeffreys

-1-

Jimmy Blake was returning home to his hometown of Misetown, twenty-five years after leaving to pursue a career in photography.

His career had taken him the world over taking pictures of all the great things that Mother Nature had to offer and in return selling them to make his small fortune to continue travelling but now it was time to come home.

His parents had recently passed, he had no family to speak of, so it was time to maybe plant some roots back in this hometown. He had money saved and his parents had left him a few bucks, so maybe, just maybe it was time to stop living out of his suitcases.

When Jimmy passed the sign for Misetown, population 5,500, he was surprised to see the numbers had grown since he left. There wasn't much to do here and the old factory had long since closed and last he heard from his Mom, people were leaving by the numbers to find a new path, so how had the numbers grown? Must be a typo or maybe just a bad joke to attract the tourists.

Misetown wasn't a bad place to grow up but there was always something about it....it did attract the tourists due to its numerous ghost stories, as any town had....given history anywhere and rumours start to grow and the next thing you know, people are coming from far to see if those old stories are true, or to get a peak at maybe an old ghost hanging around.

Come to think of it, last time he had run into a fellow photographer on one of his travels, he had told him the stories of where he was from and Ben, he thought he was called, was intrigued enough to say he would be paying a visit to Misetown to continue writing his book on ghost towns and was hoping to snap a photo of a ghost or two to finish it up.

Jimmy wasn't sure if Ben had come or not as he hadn't heard from him since that last trip he'd been seen on, but he would be sure to ask around now that he was back in town.

-2-

Jimmy slowed his Jeep Wrangler as he pulled past the *Welcome* sign, to take in the memories that crept back....over there beside the old Hardware Store, he had his first kiss with Jenny, a grade younger but mature beyond her years at age 12. That is in fact what attracted him to her most. Her auburn hair and green eyes had nothing to do with his attraction but it sure seemed like yesterday as he looked into those eyes and wondered about a future with her, even at that age.

Sadly however, she had just packed up and left with her family, without a word and he had never heard from her, or of her again. Not even his Mom knew their whereabouts...all right after that night...or so it seemed.

That grocery store on the corner was the home of his very first job, packing up groceries for the locals. It was something that made his Dad proud; that he'd taken his own initiative to earn his own money to buy his first camera and pursue his picture taking, which had lead him around the world....he never even had a lesson, just kept taking pictures and developing them and the next thing he knew he was off and running.

There were memories everywhere he looked as he drove on to the only hotel there was in town, right on the main drag. But the one memory he had forgotten that came flooding back was the old Miller house. That house was hub of all the ghost stories when he was a kid. Rumours of anyone entering that house would never again see the light of day.....stories of children being dared into going in and the kids waiting around for their dared friend to never return.....tales of the house being sold numerous times to different owners and then they just up and left with no rhyme or reason and the bank would have to come in and set it up for re-sale again once all the paperwork had cleared.

But those were stories from his childhood, all things to rattle you, and while he had remembered the ghost stories and rumours to tell his friend Ben about, he had totally forgotten that house. The old Miller house.....and oddly enough, the *For Sale* sign was back up on the front lawn, maybe something else he'd had to ask around about now that he was back.

-3-

Jimmy pulled into the parking lot at the Grant Hotel, the only hotel that ever stood in Misetown for as long as he could remember: home to passing salesmen, tired truck drivers and the odd visitor for the night, and now he was one of them.

His parents having passed had left him with no home back here in Misetown. In their wills it was made clear that if they passed and Jimmy hadn't returned home before then, that his childhood home would be sold and the money left to him in a bank account set up for him by their lawyer. Some might find this strange but those were his parents wishes so he never questioned it when it came up after their passing, not long after each other six months ago.

Jimmy never even made it back for the funeral as he was halfway across the world at the time and by the time the lawyer tracked him down to tell him of their passing and their last will and testament, everything was done, and he was just now returning home to maybe get some closure.

Jimmy and his parents had once been close but somehow they got closer once he left home for greener pastures....he had come home a time or two to visit and it was like nothing had changed but also like they were impatient for him to leave again - like they didn't want him to settle down here, and while he had talked to them every week, he just felt like there was something they weren't telling him.

Jimmy was the only boy to Jane and Jack Blake who grew up here in Misetown. His Dad had worked the factory back in the day and was always home for dinner with Janey, as he like to call his high school sweetheart Jane, who made a living staying home for Jimmy sewing town's clothes when needed. The town seamstress she was and she was darn good at it too, as Jimmy proudly remembered.

Jimmy had the perfect family life as he recalled, embarking from his Jeep to gather his overnight bags and camera equipment to go check in to the hotel. So why had he stayed away for so long? Why had he remained on the road all these years, single and carefree? And why had his parents never wanted him home to take care of them even though he knew they loved him?

All these questions poured through him as he walked into the small lobby and up to the check-in counter, placing his bags on the floor to stand back up to face the greenest eyes and most beautiful auburn hair he had ever seen. It couldn't be...?

"Jenny?" he asked,"Jenny Cooper? It can't be?"

Jimmy's breath was taken away like he had just seen a ghost and the look on her face generated the same emotion. But as Jimmy blinked and looked again, he realized while it was Jenny, it was just a large photograph of her behind the desk of the hotel, so lifelike it had brought him back to that corner where he had shared that first kiss.

The hotel clerk came out of the backroom upon hearing Jimmy's voice and looked to where Jimmy's eyes were glued.

"Yeah, that's my granddaughter Jenny, over thirty years ago now since that photo was taken but I can't bring myself to replace it with anything else. She was my little ray of sunshine that made my every day worth living. Just can't bear to take it down, just can't do it," sighed the old gentleman behind the counter.

Jimmy gave himself a shake and turned to look at the old guy. "Mr. Cooper? Grandpa Cooper? Gosh I remember seeing you every time I walked Jenny home from school back in the day, but I thought you had moved away with Jenny and her folks?"

"Nah, I stuck around in hopes they would come back one day but so far, nothing....no letter, no word of any kind from them since they moved away. I still keep hoping but I've nowhere else to be so I stick around and look after this here hotel in hopes that one day someone will check in with some word of them. But so far, not a peep," again sighed Grandpa Cooper. "Take it you haven't heard from her, eh?"

"I wish I could say I had," said Jimmy. "I'm just back in town to maybe settle down and take a look around and find some answers. And one of those questions was about Jenny. She always was the girl of my dreams, always."

Jenny's Grandfather looked at Jimmy, more closely this time. "Jimmy Blake, well I'll be....I didn't even recognize you for a minute, but heck, look at you, all grown up. I was sure sorry to hear about your folks. Good people they were."

"Thanks. It was tough but they had a good life together and raised me well. Just wished I could have made it back in time for everything but it was done quick and the lawyer couldn't find me til it was too late but here I am now and I guess I'll see where that takes me," half smiled Jimmy, "so you got any extra rooms?"

"For the likes of you, Jimmy, I sure do," smiled Grandpa Cooper. "I sure do and let's catch up later."

Jimmy settled himself into room 201 and unpacked his two small suitcases and took out his camera to load up to get ready to head out for a trip down memory lane. He pulled on his jacket and wandered out the door and turned to the right, up the main drag to his old street, Old Mill Road, and took a left and walked up to number 26.

Not much had changed except a new paint job, maybe, and different curtains blew in the windows. As new owners had moved in about three months ago, he was told by his parents' lawyer, but aside from that, it looked like it always had. He continued his walk down to Jenny's home and stopped.

Jenny had lived on the same road as him so it was easy to walk her home but even if she had lived five miles away, he still would have walked her home, by her side - he would have followed her anywhere back then.

Jimmy came back to the present and just stared at the old house. It looked like no one had upkept her old place but there was no for sale sign anywhere to indicate that it was neglected or left behind. It just looked dark and dreary with overgrown weeds and grass, trees covering the upstairs windows and darkness emitting from the windows and half open front door. Even though it looked like no one had set foot in there for years, Jimmy didn't have the heart to enter the place, preferring to keep his happy memories of Jenny and her house for now.

Jimmy continued his walk down Old Mill Road, past the old factory, up Main Street and over to the graveyard to visit his folks. He walked through the front gate and took a right to where he remembered they had purchased their plots and sat down in front of their graves. He had thought, he had cried his share of tears the day he had heard of their passing and everyday since, but seeing their headstones, only made it all the more real and opened the floodgates again.

"Oh Mom, Dad.....why didn't you tell me you were in poor health? I would have come home to care for you....I would have been here to take care of everything," Jimmy cried into his hands. "I was your only son, your only family, why?"

After Jimmy had wept a few more tears, he wiped them away and rose up and said he'd be back again tomorrow to see them.

Jimmy walked back out the gates but instead of turning to go back to the hotel, he walked across the street to go down the road a bit to Lively Way, the road of the *For Sale* sign and the old haunted house - the old Miller house.

Jimmy approached the house slowly, still afraid of the old place and the stories even though he was now an adult. He tried to shake off the feeling that someone was watching him from the house. It was just his mind playing tricks on him. There was nothing to be afraid of...it was just a house...ghosts weren't real....nothing could hurt or scare him, even though as a child, he had never came even close to this place, just in case. But now that he was older, it was fine, nothing to be afraid of.

-4-

The following morning, Jimmy awoke and went downstairs to talk to Jenny's grandfather but he was nowhere to be found. *Well, I'll come find him later*, thought Jimmy and headed out to talk to his parents' lawyer, Mr. Wilkins.

Mr. Wilkins' office was on the main street, upstairs from the old hardware store. Jimmy walked up the stairs and into the office where a reception desk was located but no receptionist. So Jimmy popped his head into the office behind and saw whom he thought was Mr. Wilkins filing away some paperwork in the drawers.

"Mr. Wilkins?" Jimmy asked, knocking on the outer door.

Mr. Wilkins turned and looked up. "Yes, how can I help you?"

"I'm Jimmy Blake," he answered. "You contacted me about my parents passing and the paperwork, so I thought I would come by to chat and see if there was anything else you hadn't mentioned or I needed to do?"

Mr. Wilkins sat down fast and looked at Jimmy with what seemed like fear but then quickly shook it off and responded: "Jimmy, I'm so sorry for your loss. Your parents were good people but why are you here? Everything was taken care of as I told you over the phone, so there was no need for you to make this long journey home."

"I had to come. Even if for myself and some closure," replied Jimmy. "It had been a while and like I said, I just wanted to come home and see if there was anything else."

Mr. Wilkins fidgeted with the picture frame on his desk, shuffled some paperwork before looking up at Jimmy and responding, "like I said, Jimmy, it's all taken care of. Nothing for you to do but carry on your merry way. Sorry you came all this way for nothing."

Jimmy couldn't help notice that the lawyer seemed nervous but couldn't put his finger on it, so instead asked, even surprising himself, "that old house over on Lively Way, the old Miller house, the one with the *For Sale* sign, anyway to find out who is showing it and how much it would be to buy it?"

The lawyer quickly jumped and knocked over the picture frame, showing a photo of what looked like the auburn haired Jenny, but it couldn't be so Jimmy put it out of his mind and looked again at Mr. Wilkins. "Well, who would I talk to?"

"Wwwell that would be me," stammered the lawyer, visibly shaken. "But why would you want to see it, let alone buy it? According to your folks, you haven't lived anywhere since you left home. Why here? Why now?"

Jimmy wished he knew but had no explanation so replied with, "maybe it's time I settle down. Maybe it's time I came home and since my home is already sold, and that for sale sign is there, I'd like to take a look at it and find out how much it is."

The lawyer seemed to stare at Jimmy for what seemed like forever before he responded. "Well, I can look up the asking price but truth be told, no one has lived there or even wanted to since that sign went up. You remember all the old stories growing up. I can find you the key to go take a look for yourself but I wouldn't recommend it. It's been untouched and unlived in for years, and no one much lives around here anymore so why would you want to stay there of all places? Why not just take your parents money and go find a new house, a new bigger city, but just not here."

Here the lawyer stopped and took a deep breath. "It's just a lot of work for your first place and with all that money, you could do better is all I'm thinking."

Jimmy looked away then back at Mr. Wilkins and said, "I just don't know but I want to. I need to. It's just something I can't explain ever since I drove into town last night. That *For Sale* sign, that house....I just gotta see it at least. I never did as a kid and now that I'm older, well I just don't know.....and whatya mean, no one much lives here? When I drove into town, the sign said the population had grown, but come to think of it, aside from you and Mr. Cooper at the hotel, I haven't seen many folks."

Shaking, the lawyer quickly fumbled in his drawer producing an old key. "This is to the old Lively House, but for the last time, heed my advice and just turn right back around and hightail it out of town and back where you came from. And that's all I got to say on the subject."

-5-

Jimmy left the lawyers without another word, key in hand and jogged back to his hotel. Mr. Cooper was still nowhere in sight so he went to his room, grabbed up his camera and started his walk over to the 66 Lively Way.

He passed no one along the way and again, slowly approached the house. It looked the same as it had the night before and the feeling of being watched still haunted him as he approached the gate. He looked around and saw no one, no neighbours, no one out walking, so took a deep breath and crossed into the yard.

Jimmy stood there on the walkway for a minute taking more deep breaths before shaking it off and walking towards the front door of the house. He took the key out of his pocket and realized he was shaking.

"For Gawd's sake Jimmy, pull yourself together, it's just a house and you're an adult. Stop your carrying on so," he whispered to himself before sliding the key into the old lock.

It took a few tugs but finally the lock clicked and the door was ready to open but Jimmy wasn't ready to open it....."Stop it," he said as he put his hand on the knob and turned it to open the door.

Before Jimmy crossed the threshold, he couldn't help but feel something familiar and safe but at the same time, a warning....a threat to turn around and go back, do not enter came to mind, and he almost listened, feeling a cold chill from somewhere inside the house. Nonsense, it's all nonsense, he muttered to himself as he entered into the house.

The house was dark even though it was light out and it smelled old, maybe dank, damp....what was that smell? Jimmy couldn't be sure as felt along the wall for a light switch.

Finding none, Jimmy took out his camera and grabbed the flash to give him more light, it seemed the flash went off bright in his face by itself, then nothing. As he felt along the walls, past the entrance, and further into the house, he had that feeling again of being watched but this time from inside the house.

Finally getting further enough in the house and feeling a light switch, Jimmy slid his hand to the on position and turned on the light, but when he turned, he quickly dropped and fell to his knees. For there on the wall, were thousands and thousands of photos in frames and it looked to Jimmy like they were all staring right at him.

Jimmy slowly got up to take a closer look and as he approached the first set of frames, he couldn't help but see that they were all head shots of people - people of every age, every walk-of-life, male and female, old and young, and as he looked more closely, he realized that they looked familiar even.

Yes, they were familiar because they were the photographs of the town's people of Misetown. There was his old kindergarten teacher, Miss Winkler....his neighbours, The Browns....the town barber, Jack – yes, Jack was his name.....

As Jimmy walked from the thousands of frames in this room to every room in the house, he recognized more and more people and also some he didn't. When went upstairs to take a look at more photos, he opened the door to a room that took his breath away because on this wall....there were photos of Mr. Cooper just as he saw him yesterday, Mr. Wilkins as he saw him an hour ago, in his suit....his friend Ben, his parents pictures were here too, his Mom and Dad in separate frames side by side almost like they were terrified for him. But how could that be, they were photos?

But the picture that terrified him the most was of Jenny....his Jenny in that same blue dress he had last seen her in as he kissed her that very first and last time in front of the hardware store. She was there in a frame just staring at him, with not quite fear, but sadness too.

Jimmy slowly approached her frame and saw that her parents were in separate frames on both sides of her. As he got closer to Jenny, he could hear her whispering from inside the frame: *"Jimmy, why did you have to come? We've all tried to keep you away from Misetown, from this house....your parents, especially me, with Mr. Wilkins and my Grandpa. Why did you have to come? Now you can never leave."*

Jimmy looked around the room at all the familiar faces of people he once knew and now their expressions had all changed to sadness. Jimmy looked back at Jenny's picture and asked, "Wwwhat do you mean? I can never leave?"

It was almost like Jenny reached out to take his hand from the frame and said, *"Jimmy, none have ever left. We've all been tricked into this house one way or another, me as a child after that night we first kissed. I was enticed in by the sound of a mewing kitten and been stuck here since. My parents came looking for me and heard my voice from inside the house and came in, to never leave again. Even your parents....my Grandfather, Mr. Wilkins....they're all here, forever, stuck in this house."*

Jimmy stammered, "but how, I don't understand....I just saw your Grandfather yesterday at the hotel and Mr. Wilkins at his office this morning, how is that possible? This doesn't make any sense."

"My Grandfather and Mr. Wilkins were only allowed out to let you see people here, if you recall, you didn't see my Grandpa again after and you probably didn't see anyone else out in Misetown either," Jenny continued, *"this house has a curse....anyone who enters has their soul taken away and put into a frame forever along with their photo and I'm afraid, it's now the same for you, Jimmy. When you came in, you saw a flash....that was your photo being taken and your soul now in a frame for all time, I'm sorry Jimmy."*

Jimmy tried to look around but couldn't any longer. He could only look ahead at Jenny, as she was on that last day....in her blue dress....across the room from him in her frame, staring at her from his frame....forever.

Beautiful Killer
by Summer Breeze

Its veins were bright blue; I could see them pulsing through the green iridescent wings as it sucked the life from its victim. The rigid proboscis was rammed down the man's throat, sucking up fluids faster than he could gasp, or even choke, around it. Now a horrible parasite upon the earth, the butterflies had mutated to this size and form through our own quest for immortality. Some would say through our own destructive tendencies, for look how all the genetic tampering had turned out: instead of living forever we were dying faster, and by the thousands.

"We'll choose something harmless," they'd said. "Something fragile - beautiful to behold - and see if we can't make it stronger, indestructible." If it worked with something as insubstantial as that, they'd reasoned, then surely it would only be a matter of time before it worked for us.

Well, it had worked all right. Too well. And the creatures had escaped because, as usual, we hadn't thought it all through properly. The tests on their food source hadn't quite turned out as expected. The plants had grown bigger but the drastic alterations had destroyed something vital, something the butterflies needed. They couldn't sustain themselves without a natural environment. Frantic to find food, the butterflies had destroyed the specially designed greenhouse, their now-hardened wings slicing through the glass walls of their prison as if it were no more substantial than cobweb.

Human skin proved equally fragile, and blood soon flowed freely. The creatures quickly lapped it up and developed a liking for it; after all, it was the only nutritious fluid available to them at the time, and the screaming throats of scientists, researchers and workers looked remarkably like the tubes of certain flowers...

The world hadn't been the same since.

Now we hid, flitted from bush to bush for cover. Our homes weren't safe anymore. Some people migrated in groups as the new threat to our existence had once done, but they were taking a great risk in doing so; the insects were still nearsighted, still tended to race toward clumps of food rather than a single source. We'd forgotten to dampen their ability to breed, so they were plentiful, and it was nothing for them to form a swarm within seconds and overpower humans ignorant of their habits. The old adage of safety in numbers no longer held true.

Of course we weren't much safer on our own either. Being less of a temptation didn't mean the insects couldn't sense the vibration of your movements on the wind with their wings, or pick up your scent through their feet or antennae if you strayed too close. The females had gone and done one better: they'd learned to pick up our alarm pheromones. Don't exist, you say? Yeah, yet another theory we'd been more right than wrong about but hadn't taken any further. It was no longer safe to sweat.

Personally, I masked my sweat with the spoils of my first kill. Purely by accident I had learned that the adult versions still had soft spots: where their legs met their thorax and where their heads were attached to their bodies. They didn't need to swivel them to see you, but if you were very lucky you could catch them while they were eating as I had done. Then it was a matter of driving a long kitchen knife into the back of their neck, slicing until the head fell off, and smearing yourself in their scent. I found a leg was easier to carry in my pack so I went with that. Besides, the large hook that served as a foot turned out to be better than any kitchen knife I could scrounge.

It tore through wings, too. Of course it took great strength to do any of that. Ironically, my strength came from them. One day, in an attempt to learn more about my enemy - and subsequently how better to kill it I'd stolen one of their eggs. (They were everywhere now, so it wasn't a difficult task.) The shell had been impossibly hard. So hard in fact, that banging it with a rock had produced no result, but fortunately not so hard that another egg couldn't smash it open like the regular chicken variety. I'd ended up covered in it. Inside it was sticky - not fluid, but enough to make it difficult to get out of my mouth, which I'd opened in reflex. I couldn't help but swallow some of it, though I tried not to. I studied closely then killed the unhatched larvae, surprised to discover it wasn't all that difficult; suddenly I had new strength in my limbs. I tested my teeth on a piece of shell and found it to be delicious - like spun sugar.

Since then I'd killed many larvae and had eaten many a shell. I carried small pieces in my pack all the time for when hunger overtook me. I was constantly on the move, so this was more practical than trying to cook something my fellow humans had left behind.

I had also tried to kill pupa. If you caught the emerging butterfly while hatching and still vulnerable it was fairly easy, but the adults had gotten smart now and slept amongst them. So lately I hadn't found many in that state.

I peeked out of the split in the abandoned chrysalis I now occupied. (They were great for sleeping in - warm, and safe.) Finally, the insect was finished with the poor man. It withdrew its velvet sword from his torn throat, curling it underneath a chin, bristling with needle-like hairs, and dropped the empty husk of humanity like so much garbage. The horror of such a sight still hadn't lessened and I swallowed - a reassurance of sorts that my own throat still functioned properly. I needed to watch the insect take off and fly, to learn what I would need to do to do the same. My plan was to cut a pair of wings from the back of one of them and use them to attack other butterflies from above. If I could do it I could pass the information on to others. We could eat the insects' eggshells, blend in with the adults, smell like them and destroy them one by one. Maybe save more humans from an ending like the one I'd just witnessed. Then travelling in packs would start to be a benefit, instead of just suicidal.

I huddled inside my covering, and waited.

Demon Hunter
by Allan McCarville

June, 1853

When he woke this morning, if Preston Hughes had known he'd be skulking through fog enveloped woods at the edge of a cemetery at midnight, he likely would not have bothered to get out of bed.

However, it was too late now to back out of the deal he had made. The money Dr. Henry Barnes had offered was just too good to turn down, even if the job was illegal. Now that he found himself actually approaching the cemetery, the pay that sounded so generous with alcohol infused thinking was suddenly far less appealing.

He paused and listened.

All was quiet, aside from the hooting of a lone owl somewhere in the trees. He peered into the shadows, and through the gloom he could distinguish where the trees thinned out, and he could perceive the silhouette of the iron fence that marked the rear boundary to the graveyard. He set his lantern down behind a tree where he would recover it on the return journey. A light in the cemetery at this time of night risked attracting unwanted attention.

He began walking again, now carrying only a shovel. The feeble moonlight cast just enough light through the night mist to illuminate his path with a murky silver-grey radiance.

He reached the fence and effortlessly climbed over. The fence wasn't very high; its purpose was to mark a boundary, not to prevent anyone from entering.

Inside the graveyard, he looked around and saw the stone storage shed where the caretaker kept all his tools. Spread out across the front of the shed, and to its right-hand side, Preston saw neat rows of headstones. While some of them were beginning to show signs of aging, none had as yet toppled over, although a few were tilting at a precarious angle.

Preston was not interested in that part of the cemetery.

His destination was to the left side of the shed, the side where the town of Bridgewater buried paupers and criminals. The unknown, the unwanted, cast into unmarked graves. A few of those graves had crosses, others were marked with a temporary wooden stake that would not last the first winter. But most had nothing aside from a shallow depression to mark the final resting place of some forgotten soul.

The grave he was after was easy to find. A mound of freshly turned earth marked the spot; the occupant had only been laid to rest that morning. There was just enough moonlight to read the inscription on the wood stake:

David Young. Thief. Died 21 June 1853.

This was the body Dr. Barnes wanted. Young had died only yesterday. Preston hadn't asked why Barnes wanted Young's body; it was none of his concern. Preston was acquainted with Young, but they were not close friends, although they had shared an ale from time to time. While Young would not be joining him for any more tankards, the money Preston would make from his corpse would keep *him* in ale for several weeks to come.

He shivered involuntarily as he steeled himself for what he had to do.

That's when he heard the noise.

Preston froze, looked around, and at first saw nothing. He focused his gaze on the caretakers shed and squinted into the mist. *Was that someone standing beside the shed?* He blinked and the figure was gone.

Just my imagination, he told himself with more hope than conviction. He stood by the new grave and glanced furtively around. He saw nothing; the only sound he heard was the fear induced drumming of his own heart. He swallowed nervously, took a deep breath, then started digging.

Digging up the grave was easier than he anticipated as the earth had not had time to settle. He soon reached the roughly made coffin and he paused to catch his breath. He was straddling the box and he suddenly wondered how Young had died. Barnes had told him little, aside from the fact the man had died in the county jail.

Unfortunately, Preston had been too drunk and too focused on the amount of money he would make to question the cause of Young's demise. Preston shook his head. How the man died was irrelevant. Dead is dead.

He mopped his brow with his handkerchief before tying it around his mouth, hoping that it would prevent him from breathing in any sickness that might be lingering in the coffin. He used the shovel to pry open the lid then apprehensively looked at the mortal remains of David Young. He was relieved to discover that the body was completely wrapped in a sheet.

The last thing he wanted to see was Young's corpse staring back at him.

Now came the hard part. Young had been short and lean, whereas Preston was tall and muscular. Nevertheless, it was no easy task manoeuvring the body out of the box and lifting it out of the grave.

Once the body was out, Preston hoisted himself out of the hole then collapsed beside the corpse to catch his breath.

A sound reached him, a low barely audible moan. Again, he peered into the gloom but saw nothing. *The wind*, he thought, *just the wind*. Nevertheless, a sense that he was being watched washed over him.

It was definitely time to go.

Preston struggled but managed to lift the body and drape it over his shoulder. Young might not have been big, but lifting his dead weight was challenging. Walking awkwardly, he left the graveyard. Getting Young over the fence was difficult but he managed, and it was with enormous relief that he spotted his lantern.

The return journey stumbling through the woods to where he had left his horse and cart took almost twice as long as the walk in. Finally reaching the cart, he deposited the body in the back and took a final look around before climbing up onto the driver's bench. He saw no one, but the feeling that he was being watched prevailed.

It took all his self-control not to urge the horse into a gallop. Racing along the dirt road in the dark was a disaster in the making. Nevertheless, he kept the animal at a brisk walk, constantly glancing over his shoulder, searching for whoever or whatever that he was certain was following him.

His pent-up tension drained out of him when the trees and open fields gave way to Bridgewater's shops and houses as he made his way into town. He guided the horse and cart through the empty streets, slowly making his way to the alley next to the tavern where Dr. Barnes was supposed to be waiting.

He reached the entrance, pulled the cart to a stop and climbed down from the bench. He stared into the alley but it was still too dark to see more than a few paces in, and he felt panic rise up at the possibility that Barnes would not show up. He couldn't very well drive around town with a body in his cart.

"Right on time," declared a voice behind him.

Preston almost had a heart attack at the sudden appearance of his client. "Dr. Barnes," he gasped.

Barnes walked to the cart and peeled back the sheet covering the body's head. Preston caught an unintentional glimpse of Young's unnaturally pale face. Dr. Barnes nodded his approval, reached into his pocket, took out a wad of bills, and passed them over to Preston.

"Here's your money," he said. "Feel free to count it."

Preston just took the money and shoved it into his coat pocket without counting. He just wanted to get rid of the body and get home.

Barnes signalled down the alley and two men appeared. They were young, dressed as labourers, but they lacked the skin tone acquired with spending hours outside. They silently pulled the body from the back of the cart and disappeared back down the alley. They likely had another conveyance out of sight that they would use to secretly transport the body to wherever Dr. Barnes told them.

"You've done well, Preston Hughes," stated Barnes. "I look forward to doing business with you again in the future."

Preston vigorously shook his head. He was done with grave robbing, even if he made the equivalent of two months wages for a night's work. "No," he declared vehemently "I'll not rob another grave for ye."

He climbed onto the cart's bench and snapped the reins. Barnes's humourless laughter following him as he raced for home.

Home for Preston was a small cabin just outside the town limits where he lived alone. By the time he arrived, the horizon had gone from deep blue-black to a golden yellow, heralding the start of a new day. He quickly unharnessed the horse, fed and watered it, then sprinted to the house. He entered the kitchen, locking the door behind him, grateful that the unpleasant job was done.

Preston Hughes was no saint. He had done many illegal things in his life, but this was his first grave robbery. He vowed it would be his last.

He took down a bottle and glass from the cupboard beside the sink and poured himself a full measure. He gulped it down, then with hands that were still shaking, poured himself another. He exhaled a huge sigh of relief; he was safe.

He grabbed the bottle and headed for the parlour. Morning sunshine had brightened the room but it was still unexpectedly chilly. He added kindling to the fireplace, lit it, and when it caught, he added a couple of logs. He held his hands over the fire but despite the blaze, the room just wouldn't warm up.

Something creaked. He spun around and stared in terror at the figure sitting in his armchair.

David Young stared back at him.

Preston was paralyzed and could only watch as Young raised a finger and pointed it accusingly. Young's eyes began to glow, first light yellow, then bright green then, finally, blazing red.

Preston felt a burning sensation in his chest and realized he would never get to spend the money Barnes had paid him.

* * *

Present Day

The man studied his reflection in the mirror and saw the telltale signs of degradation. It was starting. No one else would be able to see the tissue degeneration for another several days, but once it began, the process accelerated.

It was time to return to Bridgewater and initiate a new cycle.

He could already feel the stirrings of the entity that empowered his quest for vengeance against the town that had condemned him for a crime he did not commit. He would get his revenge and continue to live; the entity would collect more souls, gain more power.

Every twenty-four years.

That's how old he was when he died almost 168 years ago. Even after all this time, the hatred and rage that he had felt as his life ebbed away in the town gaol burned as hot now as it did then.

Ironically, the town responsible for his death was also the source of his immortality. As he had laid dying in that cell, cursing the town, a voice offered him the opportunity to exact revenge. At first, he thought the voice was merely a figment of his imagination, something created by his dying brain.

Now he knew differently.

He smiled as he tilted his head slightly so that he could see the reflection of his other self, the entity. There was a time when that image frightened him. Not anymore. Now he welcomed it.

Tomorrow he would drive to Bridgewater. Once there, he would give himself over to the control of the thing in the mirror.

He could already feel the urge beginning to burn inside him, the craving for revenge so strong he could almost taste it. By the time the summer solstice arrived, his need to kill would be so compelling he would be unable to stop himself, even if he wanted to.

Which he didn't.

* * *

The young man parked the rental car in a vacant slot in front of the library, and slid out from behind the wheel, a backpack slung over one shoulder. He fed enough coins into the meter to pay for a couple of hours, which he considered should be sufficient, at least to start.

It was hot and humid, his shirt stuck to his body. He glanced up at the sky where he saw the tall, roiling cumulonimbus clouds that were the harbingers of an impending storm.

There was definitely a storm approaching, but not just the one the sky was threatening.

He mounted the wide stone steps leading up to the library's broad wooden doors. He glanced around before pulling them open, but there was no obvious sign of what he was searching for. He was hoping he wouldn't see any signs, which suggested there was still time.

A welcoming wall of cool air greeted him as he crossed the threshold. He took a few seconds to enjoy the relief from the humidity, then approached the reception desk where a young woman regarded him with a smile.

"Good afternoon," she said. "Welcome to the Bridgewater Library. Are you interested in signing up for a library card?"

"How do you know I don't already have one?" he asked her, his lips curling up into a hint of a smile.

The young woman's smile turned into a small laugh. "Bridgewater's not that big a town," she told him. "I know most people who use the library on a regular basis and I don't recall seeing you before. Therefore, I'm presuming that you're new."

"Guilty as charged," admitted the young man raising his arms in a gesture of surrender.

"So, will you be needing a library card?" she repeated.

The young man shook his head. "No. Actually, I'm only here for a few days on a special assignment," he informed her. "I need to conduct some research and thought I would start with the library. I don't plan to take out any books, just check some of the old newspapers and such."

"No, you won't need a card for that," confirmed the woman, "but you'll still need to sign in."

"Thank you, Ms. Grace Elliot," he said.

The woman's eyes widened in surprise. "How did you know my name?"

The man grinned and indicated the name plate on the desk.

"Oh," giggled an embarrassed Grace. "Most people don't pay any attention to it so I forget it's there." Blushing slightly, she reached into a drawer beneath the counter and placed a form on the desktop along with a pen. "If you would just complete this form then I'll take you back to our archives, Mr....?" Grace arched her eyebrows with the unspoken question.

"My name is Michael Sinclair," said the young man as he accepted the form and began to fill it out.

Grace studied Sinclair thoughtfully. She guessed he was in his mid-twenties, the same age as she was, give or take a year. He was definitely handsome, not overly tall, maybe a few inches shy of six feet, but was lean and fit as near as she could tell. He wasn't muscular, but she sensed he harboured an innate power that was both awe-inspiring and maybe even a little frightening.

"So what research are you doing, Mr. Sinclair," she asked.

He looked up from the form and smiled at her. "Please call me Michael. I feel old when people refer to me as Mr. Sinclair." He completed the form, signed it and passed it back. "I'm looking at some background information on one of Bridgewater's urban legends."

Grace's face lit with interest. "Which one are you interested in?"

"David Young," was all he had to say and he could tell immediately that Grace was aware of the story, or at least the more popular version. He doubted anyone really knew the truth about the entity behind the legend.

"Ah, yes," she said, confirming his suspicion that she was aware of the story. "We have a lot of material collected over the years, but I can give you a bit of background."

"Please, do," said Michael. "I'm more interested in the earliest beginning of the legend. As legends grow, the facts sometimes get distorted."

"Well, David Young was accused of theft and was being held in the town jail waiting for his trial," she began. "Unfortunately, he got sick and died. It was later learned that he hadn't stolen anything. Some say that the last meal they gave him was poisoned and some think it was the town doctor that did it, but it was never proven."

Michael smiled his encouragement for her to continue. So far, the information she provided matched his own.

"Anyway," continued Grace, "poor David was buried in an unmarked grave in the old cemetery. Legend has it that the town doctor hired a man named Preston Hughes to dig up the remains."

"Why would he do that?" wondered Michael.

Grace shrugged her shoulders. "It was never proven, but my grandfather told me that Doc. Barnes was selling cadavers and organs to a college in the capitol. In those days it was the only way medical schools could get a body for studying. Barnes had connections with the medical school and it was rumoured that he didn't always wait for some poor soul to die naturally. Anyway, long story short, Young's grave was unearthed and his body taken. Next day both Hughes and Dr. Barnes were found dead, but Young's body was never recovered."

"Are they certain it didn't end up at the medical school?" asked Michael.

Grace shrugged and shook her head. "Apparently not. It certainly didn't end up in the classroom, and the college was searched when it was discovered how Dr. Barnes earned his extra income. I suppose the medical school might have quietly buried it because there was quite a scandal at the time," she suggested.

"So, what's the legend say?" inquired Michael.

"They say that Young's body was never found because he came back to life," Grace answered. "He was twenty-four when he supposedly died. It's said that every twenty-four years he returns to take revenge on the town."

"What sort of revenge?" asked Michael.

"He randomly kills townsfolk," she replied. "They are killed in terrible manners, some are beheaded, others have their hearts ripped out, terrible mutilations."

"Sounds pretty dreadful," remarked Michael.

"Very," agreed Grace. "Come follow me. I'll take you to our archives."

Grace led him past shelves of books to the back of the library where she ushered him into a small room equipped with several monitors attached to microfiche readers. "All our local newspapers have been copied onto microfilm," she explained. She pointed to a shelf with several dozen small boxes lined up. "They're all there," she said. "The reels are arranged chronologically. We just ask that when you're done with a reel, you rewind it and put it back. If you want to print off any pages, come see me and I'll set it up. Just be aware that we charge a quarter for each page. If you have a thumb drive, you can transfer the data onto the drive."

"Thank you, Grace," said Michael. "You've been very helpful." He watched her as she left the room to return to her post at the reception desk. He sighed wistfully at the pleasant thoughts evoked by the affable young woman. Sadly, as much as he would like it, given his ability and the responsibility that came with it, long-term relationships simply were not possible.

Pushing thoughts of Grace from his mind, Michael threw himself into reviewing the dozens of reels, his backpack, with its precious contents, never far from his reach.

After several hours, he leaned back in his chair and rubbed his tired eyes. He was now convinced that the legend was true, at least the parts that he would have to deal with. He also knew he had less than twenty-four hours to prepare and he would need help. He glanced around and checked that the door was securely closed. He had to make a call and didn't want anyone listening in on this conversation.

"It's me, Michael," he advised the person who answered. "I need to speak with Father Paul. It's urgent."

There was a moment of silence before a man's voice came across. "Father Paul here," he said. "Is that you Michael?"

"It is, Father," verified Michael. "I'm pretty certain that what we suspected is true. We have a demon operating in this area. It's a spirit thief that controls the body of a man named David Young."

"Are you sure?" asked Father Paul although he knew that if Michael Sinclair said there was a demon on the loose, there was no doubt.

"Yes," replied Michael. "David Young had been falsely accused of theft plus he was murdered while in jail waiting for his trial. His alleged killer was the town doctor, who had a sideline business of providing cadavers to medical schools and apparently was not above hastening the demise of someone to meet the demand."

"So, it's likely that Mr. Young was full of hate and rage when he passed, which would make him susceptible to demonic possession if offered a shot at revenge," observed Father Paul.

"That's what I believe," agreed Michael.

"We need to send that demon back to Hell," said Father Paul, "and free the souls it has entrapped. How many souls has it captured?"

"Nineteen by my count," answered Michael. "I've checked the records. Although the legend suggests that young kills victims by some rather brutal means, in fact all the deaths I attribute to the demon would not attract media or police attention. Heart attacks or accidents. It's only when you look at the details would you notice that those deaths are odd. Heart attacks in young healthy people, accidents that are really bizarre, etc."

"Pattern?" asked Father Paul.

"Every twenty-four years," Michael advised him. "All during the summer solstice."

"The summer solstice is the day after tomorrow," observed Father Paul.

"Which is why we need to act quickly," said Michael.

Michael could hear Father Paul as he hummed and hawed, the elderly priest mentally reviewing the short list of operatives at his disposal. Michael was special, as were the others who Father Paul engaged. They were amongst the very few people who possessed the extremely rare ability to detect demons. Obviously, it was an ability that none of them openly admitted to, given that most people didn't believe demons even existed. Considering the time frame before the solstice, the list of available operatives was very short. In fact, Michael had a pretty good idea of who was on that list and it didn't make him happy.

"There's only two who can be with you within the next twenty-four hours," said Father Paul, confirming Michael's fears.

"Cathy and Thomas," guessed Michael reluctantly, naming his sister and brother.

"I know you don't like exposing them," said Father Paul, "but both have demonstrated their ability."

"Thomas is only a kid," Michael reminded him.

"I know," responded Father Paul. "I wouldn't send him if the situation wasn't urgent, but we need to stop that demon. Unfortunately, he and Cathy are the nearest and it takes three to form the triangle, the trinity, to confine and trap the demon and destroy it."

Michael released an exasperated sigh and once again wondered what he and his two siblings had done to be cursed with this ability. Until that terrible night, they had been a normal family, living on the farm that had been in the family for four generations. Then a strange light appeared in the barn in the wee hours of the morning. They went to investigate and something emerged, something that was evil and defied description. It attacked and destroyed the house, killing his parents in the process. Michael, Cathy, and Thomas had sought refuge in the barn, where they were exposed to that strange light. Ever since, they could sense the presence of evil.

They also had the power to destroy it.

Michael was nineteen at the time, Cathy was sixteen and Thomas only nine. That was three years ago.

No one believed their story, of course, and the authorities were convinced that Michael, and perhaps even Cathy, were behind their parents' death. Both Michael and Cathy were being held on suspicion of murder, and Thomas had been placed in the care of the local child protection services.

That's when an elderly priest, Father Paul Kennedy, arrived. Michael and Cathy had no idea where he came from, but he somehow managed to save them from the clutches of well-intentioned but misguided authorities. He ferreted them away to a remote convent where they met a few others who had suffered through similar experiences.

"We'll be there by noon tomorrow," Father Paul told him.

"Okay," acknowledged Michael unhappily, then he disconnected.

He rewound the various reels and placed them back in their containers before returning them to their place on the shelf in accordance with Grace's instructions. He had a lot of work to do before his siblings arrived, but his first order of business was doing something about the hunger pangs that gnawed at his stomach. He thought about Grace and smiled. Long-term relationships were not in the cards for him, but dinner engagements certainly worked.

* * *

The following night found Michael, his sister, and brother, along with Father Paul at Bridgewater's old cemetery. It was still very humid, but at least the rain had held off.

Lightning lit up the night sky, thunder rumbling ominously like an approaching locomotive. Twelve-year-old Thomas flinched at the noise as he walked behind his older brother and sister, with Father Paul behind him. Each of them was carrying a backpack. Michael was leading them further into the overgrown cemetery that had not been used in over fifty years.

"There's the old caretaker's shed," whispered Michael hoarsely, pointing to a bulky dark shadow. "The spot we want is somewhere over there. That's where they used to bury the paupers and criminals."

They cautiously made their way to the desolate space, mindful that they were walking over the graves of individuals who had died over two centuries earlier. When they were approximately in the middle, Michael turned and looked down at his younger brother.

"Okay, Thomas. Do your thing," he instructed.

Thomas slid his backpack off his slim shoulders, passed it to Michael, then closed his eyes. He slowly turned in a circle, then stopped and opened his eyes. Ignoring Father Paul and his siblings, he began walking slowly away from them, then stopped and closed his eyes again. Once again, he turned in a slow circle before he stopped and inclined his head to one side as if listening to something only he could hear. He opened his eyes and began walking that direction for a few paces, then stopped and repeated the ritual.

Michael and Cathy silently followed their brother while Father Paul stayed where he was, keeping an eye open for unexpected visitors. The summer solstice had arrived and tonight Young would be the instrument that allowed the demon to steal souls. However, the ritual required that Young, and ultimately the demon that possessed him, to first return to the spot where Young's body had been initially interred. They didn't know why, but Father Paul suspected it might have something to do with renewing whatever vow was made all those years ago.

Of course, locating an empty unmarked grave that was over a hundred and fifty years old would have been impossible if not for the siblings' ability to sense spots where evil events had occurred. Thomas was especially adept at sensing such locations, so the task of pinpointing the long-forgotten grave fell to him.

Thomas was beginning to perceive the presence of evil. As he made his way past the rows of graves, most were benign, but a few he sensed held the bodies of people who, when they were alive, had not been very nice. However, none of those emitted the aura of pure evil that would only radiate from a spot that had hosted demonic activity.

Then it hit him like a punch in the gut. His stomach wretched and he fell to his knees choking and gasping for air. He felt himself being lifted up and away from the spot, and the nausea vanished almost as quickly as it came.

"I hate that part," he growled as his sister passed him a bottle of water.

"You did good, Thomas," said Michael, ruffling his brother's hair.

Michael stepped onto the spot where Thomas had detected the residue of demonic activity and he also experienced a sense of nausea, but much milder than what his brother had been subjected to. He was not nearly as sensitive to residual evil as Thomas.

Michael worked quickly. He extracted a spray can from his backpack and marked a three-foot circle on the spot where Thomas had fallen. He marked the centre of the circle with several stones and stepped back as the circle disappeared. He then took out a compass and paced off ten steps to the north where he sprayed an "x." He used several sticks to mark the sport before the "x" disappeared. He returned to the centre of the circle, then took ten paces to the south-east and repeated the process to the south-west, each time marking an "x." When he had finished, the spots he had marked formed the apexes of a triangle, with the circle in the middle.

That was where they needed David Young to be when they confronted him.

"Okay, take your positions," commanded Father Paul. Michael and Father Paul made their way over to the old stone caretaker's shed while Cathy and Thomas headed for the woods that butted against the boundary of the cemetery. Now all they could do was wait.

The stone shed was no longer used; the roof had collapsed decades earlier and a gaping black hole denoted where there used to be a door. Michael and Father Paul slipped inside just as the sky opened up. The shed protected them from being spotted, but it did nothing to protect them from the torrential downpour that burst upon them.

After an hour, Michael began to worry that perhaps they had misinterpreted the information, that their assumptions regarding David Young were erroneous and there was no demonic involvement.

Then he saw the figure.

At first it was difficult to make it out because of the rain, but the occasional flash of lightening provided enough illumination to identify that someone was making their way through the gravesite. The figure reached the spot that Michael had marked and stopped and stared up into the sky, both arms raised. It shouted something but Michael couldn't make out either the language or what was said, the words drowned out by the increasing peels of thunder.

"Let's move," ordered Father Paul.

He and Michael purposely made their way to the "x" closest to the shed without the figure noticing, its attention seemingly focused on the heavens. Michael detected movement from the woods, relieved to see that Cathy and Thomas were also moving to their positions.

Their movement also caught the attention of the figure they believed to be the possessed body of David Young. The process of decay had already begun, the flesh clinging to a skeleton, the suit it was wearing doing nothing to hide the horror beneath.

"Come closer, humans," called the thing posing as Young, its voice surprisingly strong. Its attention was focused on Cathy and Thomas, not yet aware of Michael and Father Paul approaching behind it. Thomas reached the "x" that marked the northern tip of the triangle while Cathy continued to the next one.

The figure pointed at Cathy. "I will take you first," it announced. It turned back to Thomas, and added, "Then I'll consume you, boy."

"I don't think so," shouted Michael.

The creature quickly turned to face Michael and made a snarling sound when it noticed Father Paul. "A priest will not save you," it declared, raising its arm to point at Michael. The figure was now more skeletal than flesh, and a yellow glow smouldered within its eye sockets.

Father Paul stepped forward and held up a crucifix. "*Daemon. Per Dei potentiam te mando ut redeas unde venisti,*" he intoned. "*Demon. By the power of God, I command thee to return to the place from whence you came.*"

"Now guys," yelled Michael. The three siblings dropped to their knees, each taking a cloth wrapped bundle out of their backpack. They unravelled the cloth to expose the simple wooden cross within, and each placed it at their "x."

"*Daemon. Per potentiam Dei, mando tibi ut redeas ad locum unde exivi,*" they chanted, adding their voices to Father Paul's invocation.

Suddenly, flame erupted from each of the crosses and three lines of fire raced to the circle where the figure stood. The figure erupted into flames, and in mere seconds all that remained was a skeleton held up by the power of a demon.

"*Daemon. Per potentiam Dei, mando tibi ut redeas ad locum unde exivi,*" shouted Father Paul stepping closer to the column of flame in the middle of the circle.

A black cloud emerged from the skeleton, hissing and gyrating, then with a final howl of hate it plunged into the earth. The skeleton, no longer held up by the power of the demon, collapsed into a pile of bones.

Then there was silence, broken only by the now distant peels of thunder. The rain had stopped; the storm had moved on.

Translucent figures appeared – nineteen of them. They regarded the bones before turning their attention to Father Paul and the others. An eerie silence fell over the cemetery, then they vanished.

"Those were his victims, weren't they?" said Cathy, making more of a statement than a question.

"Yes," replied Father Paul. "They've been freed." He looked at the three siblings. "I think we better clean up here and disappear. I don't want to be around to answer any questions when they find this pile of bones."

Morning was just breaking over the horizon by the time they had removed the last traces of their presence. The sky was still overcast, but there were patches of blue in the distance, holding out the promise that this day might be better than the previous one.

"Let's get something to eat," suggested Thomas as they climbed into the car. "I'm hungry."

"You're always hungry," observed Cathy, putting her arm around his shoulder and giving him a quick hug.

Two hours later, they had checked out of their motel and had fed and watered Thomas who declared he was now good to go. The route to the airport took them past the library that was just opening up for the day.

"Can we stop here for a minute?" asked Michael. "I just want to say goodbye to Grace. We had an enjoyable dinner last night."

"I can't believe a tightwad like you actually paid for her dinner," Cathy chided him.

"It was worth it," countered Michael as they pulled up in front of the library.

He was about to get out when Thomas stopped him. "Wait!"

Thomas closed his eyes and seemed to be listening to something. After a minute he placed his hands on his brother's shoulders. "Michael. Please don't go in there. Something's not right."

Michael twisted in his seat to look at his brother behind him.

"Please," pleaded Thomas.

Michael frowned in irritation and scowled at his younger brother. He and Grace did have a good time, and he really wanted to see her again. Then he reconsidered; there was really no hope for any meaningful relationship.

He sighed in resignation and nodded at Father Paul. "Okay. Drive on," he said unhappily.

Inside the library, Grace had seen the car pull up and recognized Michael Sinclair in the front seat. She hoped he would come in, but was not really surprised when the car drove away.

"Maybe next time, Michael," she said to herself. She knew there would be a next time, of that she had no doubt. She knew they had banished the demon possessing David Young, she had felt its rage as it left. Michael was a demon hunter, and their paths were destined to cross again.

She glanced at her reflection in the window, then turned slightly so she could view her other self and smiled at what she saw.

There was only room for one demon in this town.

Running Water
by Michel Weatherall

There was a time I hated winter. It wasn't the cold, I could handle that. It was the dark I couldn't deal with. Dark by 3:30 pm? No, thank you. Summer used to be my season. Barbeques. The long days. Those late summer evenings. Bonfires.

My wife couldn't handle the summer heat. Winter was her time. At least, that was before *The Wandering*... I now have no idea where she is.

Now I hate the summer. You can't stay indoors. Since no air conditioning unit functions anymore, there's no reprieve. The heat is stifling. But you can't go outside either. It reeks. It always reeks. Difficult to breathe. A constant putrid stench. There's no escaping it. Carrion. Like spectral tendrils, the stench would weave and reach up. You'd think a breeze would clear them away; that a strong wind would cleanse the dog days of summer. But you'd be wrong. It only brought a different miasma from a different place.

And then there's the real danger. *The Wanderers*. But I don't want to dwell on them. That problem's past now, just like that first summer.

As summer ended a different kind of death and decay gripped and crawled and clawed across the land and the city - but this time a more blessed and natural kind. Autumn.

I had originally dreaded the advent of winter. Alone and isolated, I thought I would be fearful of the coming darkness. And I was. I still didn't like the short days or early sunsets. I still hated those long cold winter nights. But I was surprised how much I enjoyed the days. I could easily and safely go outside. *The Wanderers* ceased to be a threat. A few difficult and challenging days and things became tolerable.

The first was a walk to an abandoned store for proper winter clothing, boots and a coat. The next, a trip to Home Depot; A trailer and gas generator. At first the trips were anxiety filled, the snow-clogged sidewalks and boulevards and streets and avenues were littered with what appeared as mannequins, hauntingly posed and frozen in various states of shambling gaits and stumbling walks. Some fallen over, broken on the ground, their exposed parts blessedly hidden beneath snowdrifts.

The air was brisk and fresh. No more stench of carrion. You could afford a deep breath. The kind that fills your lungs and belly. Clean.

It's the second week of an early February deep freeze. I'm enjoying a mug of hot coffee in my early morning as I gaze out my house's front window, surveying my most recent acquisition parked in my driveway: a City of Ottawa's snowplow. Today would be my first long range excursion. I could plow through previously inaccessible roads and streets. I would check my kid's elementary school. That's where they were last June when *the plague* hit. I know, I know. It's been seven months. I don't hold very much hope. But I have to know.

Next, a supply run that should stock up my reserves for the entire winter.

I also want to drive and check out the city's downtown core. I don't know what I expect to find. People maybe? Other survivors?

I finish my coffee and zip up my winter coat. Staring absentmindedly at the truck keys in my hand as I contemplate exiting my house. It's the part I hate the most. That ever so short walk from my front door to the truck. All of ten feet. That initial shock and fear never gets old.

As I open the front door, the frigid cold stings my exposed face. I keep my eyes on the icy front step, hoping to avoid what I know is standing there waiting for me. My eyes follow the icy step to the downspout fastened to my home's brick wall. It's frozen solid. Filled will ice, backed up to the upper roof's eavestroughs. I draw a deep breath through my nostrils. It's clean and brisk. No stench. I tap my knuckles on the downspout. Rock hard and solid. Just as I thought, it is filled with ice.

Hesitantly, I slowly raise my eyes. The sky is clear blue, the sunshine bright and reflecting off the white snow, its miniature crystalline substructure glistening. And there, standing, frozen in mid-stride is Mr. Grinde.

Mr. Grinde was my mailman. He's standing on my driveway, halfway between my front door and the truck. The black of his Canada Post jacket is speckled with patches of frost and ice, broken by Canada Post insignias and badges.

His touque is missing, exposing his thinning hair. A patch of flesh slightly above his left temple has been torn or peeled off, his bare skull bleached white by the sun. I need to pass within two feet of him to get to the vehicle. It's unnerving to be this close to one of *them*.

Looking almost like a walking mummy, completely inanimate and frozen solid, a slight breeze rustles his hair, briefly startling me. The skin on his face is dessicated, dried and taunt. His lips, peeled back, gives the illusion of protruding and gnashing teeth. His chin, neck, throat and collar of his shirt are stained brown from old dried blood. However, it's Mr. Grinde's eyes that are the worst. They are clouded over cataracts, lifeless and void, their gaze permanently fixed upon my home's front door.

I continued past Mr. Grinde, not wanting to ponder too deeply upon his intentions when the bitter cold caught him unawares. Climbing up into the truck, I insert the keys and turn the ignition. The diesel engine sputters and rumbles into life, its overhead exhaust pipes coughing black plumes of smoke. My children's school is only a ten minute drive away.

* * *

I suppose I hoped for some sense of closure from my trip to the school. The elementary school was a squat single-floored building. On a bright sunny day you could see through one class window and out the other.

There were no lights on. The school had no power, no electricity, no generators. Through the smeared, grimy windows only shadows were visible. I cannot know with certainty why they were grimy or what they were smeared with. I don't want to know.

Through some trick of the light, there were moments some *things* seemed to move, or shift, or shamble within the school. Like my heart and my hopes, there was an overwhelming sense of abandoned decay about the place. There was nothing living here.

Returning home and parking the snowplow, my anxiety once again climaxed at the sight of my front driveway's ditizen. Like some kind of grotesque nightmare fuelled giant lawn ornament, Mr. Grinde is still standing there frozen in mid-stride. With his back to me I am temporarily spared looking into his face. Winter's harsh breeze cascades its fingers through his wispy hair, flapping his pant legs against his icy flesh. Two elongated snow drifts extend from his petrified boots, lost and pointing to nowhere.

Walking to my front door, I have to pass within feet of him - of *it*.

I want to avert my eyes but I can't. Promising myself only the briefest glimpse, that fleeting moment turns into a demented study. No different than a child witnessing a bog mummy at the museum exhibit, a macabre curiosity checks and balances the terror.

His facial stubble seems as real as mine, the flesh of his throat, a gooseflesh-like texture. Most of the colour has withdrawn from his face, leaving a grey-brown tone, patchy and uneven. Tiny black spots are prevalent across the windward side of his head. I can only imagine the consequence of frostbite, possibly early gangrene before he froze solid.

As I enter my warm house, I shut, lock the door, and draw the deadbolt, checking the locks twice, thrice, the thoughts of frostbite and gangrene and thawed rotting meat and flesh churning through my mind, like some sort of demented meat grinder:

Could a Canadian winter be the end of *the plague*? Is it possible this nightmare was for a single season only? Frostbit flesh would turn black and slough off. If a carcass was frozen throughout, once spring returned, its thawing would leave little but collapsed effluent, tissue, and bones.

I went to bed and as I fell into slumber my head was filled with thoughts of the end of *the Wanderers*.

* * *

For the following few weeks I had fallen into a depressed reprieve, doing little but eating, sleeping, shitting and obsessing over useless worries I had no control over. I can't remember whether it was a week or two weeks. I've lost track of time. Was I now in March?

I decided it was March 12th. Daylight Savings Time. I was done with the grey days of depression. Maybe Daylight Saving Time would brighten up my days, both figuratively and literally.

Today I will take my snowplow downtown. It will do me good. Give me a sense of purpose, like I'm a contributing member of society. Helping out. Doing good. Clearing the Queensway to downtown, opening up the downtown corridors. Somebody has to do it, right? Find other survivors. I mean, once Spring comes around and all the frozen *Wanderers* collapse into rotting piles of human effluence, once *the plague* is over, we will all have the task of rebuilding civilization, right?

I filled my thermos with hot coffee, donned my winter coat, and take my truck keys. As I opened the front door my positivity was curved and enthusiasm plummeted, falling to the ground along with my gaze. Again, I wasn't prepared for what awaited me. I didn't *want* to be prepared for Mr. Grinde.

As a distraction my eyes followed the virgin snowcovered step to the downspout hanging off the upper roof's eavestroughs. With a pronounced lack of confidence I rapped my knuckles on the aluminum downspout. It was solid. No hollow sound. Backfilled with ice. Frozen to the upper eavestroughs.

I slowly, hesitantly raised my eyes. It was an overcast day. Homogeneous grey clouds covered everything. One monochrome blanket enveloped the world. The diffused phosphorescent sunlight lit up everything yet somehow cast no shadows. The harsh light left no detail unnoticed.

Slightly warmer today, it was a wet snow that fell. Mr. Grinde stood there awaiting me. Cold. Solid. Inanimate. He glistened, a light sheen of ice coating him. Glazed like some fired ceramic monstrosity. His hair was matted and flat to his head, wettened and frozen by the rain-snow. A verglas statue.

His pant legs were solid today. Soaked with the freezing rain, then petrified by the winter cold.

Lips peeled back, pulled by the skin's desiccation, still his teeth looked like they were snapping, biting at something. His lower jaw had filled with water, draining out and overpouring, forming a slowly growing icicle down his chin.

The ice coated snow broke and *crackled* like that first breaking of a crème brûlée as I gingerly passed the mailman and made my way to the truck. My high spirits had fallen. I'm not sure whether it was the gloomy day, Mr. Grinde, or my untenable position.

The truck reverberated as it started, the quiet tiny sound of shattered ice cascading on the ground around it. The sound was haunting and surreal, only further emphasizing my sense of isolation in my silent suburban neighbourhood.

***

The temperature had dropped significantly during the day. The wet-snow turned into bitter ice-shards that the wind drove like tiny knives.

I sat in the snowplow cab, parked in my driveway, replaying the events of the day over and over in my mind. The trip downtown was a depressing, hope crushing mistake. The downtown avenues acted like windtunnels; windswept and clogged up with countless numbers of *Wanderers*. There were no survivors. There *couldn't* have been any survivors. Like an army of lifeless statues, the streets were choked with them.

I drove and plowed the streets, cleaning the accumulation of snow and ice from the derelict asphalt and cleansing away the standing frozen bodies. Like the ice and snow, so too did the frozen walking cadavers shatter and break.

Ultimately, I plowed a path from my suburban neighbourhood to the downtown core and back again. A glass-half-full kind of person would say I created a road for survivors to find me.

A glass-half-empty kind of person would say once *the Wanderers* thawed out...

The truck sputtered and shook as I turned off the ignition, my mind still churning over what I had done: *But they wouldn't, would they? Thaw out, that is?*

As I approached Mr. Grinde from the rear I could see his jacket and pants and head were coated with crystalized frost. Gone was the smooth, clear glaze coating of ice. Replaced with a semi-opaque rough layer of miniscule pointed daggers. Some water had slipped beneath the flesh of his open wound on his head - the one exposing the bone of his skull. Freezing, the water has expanded, opening the wound further, extending down to his cheek.

Covered and coated with rough ice, could a walking corpse's eyes look any more dead? Mr. Grinde's certainly did. They were soulless, his mouth and teeth freeze-framed in a gnashing bite only added to the illusion that he - *it* - was only biding its time - *waiting*.

No, no, no! I shook my head, not letting my fear and imagination get the better of me. Once the thaw came it would be over. *The Wanderers would rot and fall apart. Drop to goo and pieces. Spring would be the end.*

My fear and revulsion peaked as I passed within arm's length of Mr. Grinde. My instinct demanded that I recoil. My peace of mind demanded otherwise. Screwing my courage to the sticking point, I reached out a knuckle and struck Mr. Grinde's arm. I had expected his jacket sleeve to be cold but pliable. I was wrong. It must have been saturated with water, frozen as deeply and concretely as his body. I continued to the front door passing the frozen cadaver, my hand lightly touching the downspout. Solid. Drumming my fingers on its surface, there was no reverb through its aluminum. Just a dull dead sound.

* * *

I was lost to reprieve and withdrawal from reality for days... maybe weeks. I know not how long. Eating only because I had to, my appetite lost to depression. Sleeping only when the mindless exhaustion of inactivity captured me. Surviving but not living. The necessity of biological functions, my only drive.

It had been more than a week. The days were becoming noticeably longer. It had to have been weeks. My mind toggled between the indifference of knowing what date it was, to the needful purpose of following a calendar. I had long since abandoned the days of the week.

Listlessly I stood watching the coffee maker brew my black gold, the sound of its quiet percolation holding my attention. I intensely awaited and listened to its *finale*. When its glorious brewing was done, its symphony's *coda*, the final *drip, drip, drip*, it fell into silence.

I had little other hopes or passions or vices or interests. I felt I should applaud it as silence once again reigned... but the silenced didn't... reign that is.

Another sound - evasive, elusive - caught my attention. I cocked my head to the left, listening intently. It was subtle. Alive and playing a game of hide-and-seek with me.

It was coming from the foyer. As I followed the indistinct sound, approaching the front door it grew ever so slightly in volume. Again I stood still, listening. Pressing my ear to the front door, its volume grew ever so slightly again. It was coming from outside the house.

I cautiously drew the deadbolt, my hand drifting in a surreal slowness to the doorknob lock. Pinching and turning the switch between my thumb and finger, I unlocked the door.

I was never truly prepared for what I knew awaited me outside, again my eyes fell to the front step. The sunlight cascaded across the concrete step. The shadowed side, darker and wet with water. The sunkissed side, dry and white. The sunshine was warm and invigorating on my face. The sound was coming from the downspout. I raised my hand to the aluminum tube, bringing my knuckle to the metal and rapping. It reverberated. Hollow, empty, water cascading through the downspout.

I raised my eyes to Mr. Grinde. He wasn't there. *It* wasn't there.

My gaze froze to the horrific sound of running water.

Spirits of Strife
by Matt Lalonde

December 28, 2239
Epsilon Eridani Jump Point, Sol System

The Strife was hit by another barrage of missiles, sending shocks through the vessel.

"Captain," her shield operator's voice cut in. "Secondary hull is at forty percent and falling."

Captain Summers slammed her hand into the left armrest of her command chair. The comms channel to engineering opened, "Chief, we need to jump now!"

Chief Nells began to answer. "Singularity drive is charged," he said, "But we have other problems."

There was a large explosion in the background and the whole ship rocked. Power fluctuated and the port side of the bridge went dark.

"Chief what just happened?" the Captain yelled.

"Reactors four and five just went up. We have a massive radiation problem down here." There was a pause, "A third of the ship is without power and reactors 3 and 6 look like they might be going into a cascade meltdown." There was another pause, "We need to abandon ship sir."

"That'll be the day," she spat. "Helm, jump us to Epsilon Eridani, NOW!"

"Sir, incoming MAC shots from the *Apache*!" Hobbs yelled.

"*The Discord* is firing them as well!" Richter added.

"JUMP!" Captain Summers yelled.

The Strife was pulled into a black and purple hole in space. As it went in, the reports said that it looked like a series of explosions had broken the ship apart.

* * *

December 28, 2239
Epsilon Eridani Jump Point, Epsilon Eridani System

A purple and black tear ripped space open. Explosions blew through and quickly died in the vacuum of space. The temporary fireball was followed by the dark, cold hulk of UPD-01 *Strife*. The ship was split in half at the habitation rings as both pieces lazily exited the singularity. It came to a stop a kilometer away from the jump point, floating limp and powerless in the void of space. The screams of its crew echoed through the singularity as it shut behind the hulk.

* * *

February 3, 2240
1 Kilometer from the Epsilon Eridani Jump Point

The Authorized Mercenary Ship *Harvey* used its maneuvering thrusters to carefully enter the dark hangar bay of the Dreadnaught *Strife*. Its pilot, J.P. Matthews, touched down on the cold, powerless floor. Anchor cables shot out and connected to the floor, keeping the *Harvey* in place.

Five minutes later, the four members of the crew exited the ship.

"Alright," Sandoval said, "Matthews, Horrigan, you two head to the engineering deck. See what is salvageable and get it back to the ship." He looked at another member, "Iben and I will go to the bridge and download the logs from the war table. They should be worth a pretty penny." He looked at his clock, "2 hours. That's all we will have before we run out of portable air."

The others nodded and the four men split up.

The doors slid open, screeching as they slid into the walls. The beams of light from the men's helmets illuminated the frozen room. The two figures floated in thanks to the lack of gravity. One of them floated towards the command chair, and the frozen body that sat in it.

"Permission to come aboard Captain?" Iben asked, laughing at the frozen corpse.

"That's funny," Sandoval said. He was floating next to the war table, and was hooking up their portable power pack. "Come on you bucket of bolts," he muttered.

Iben floated towards the main windows and looked out at the stars beyond.

"Hey Sandoval," Iben commented, "Have you ever heard of Singularity Spirits?"

Sandoval was working on the war table, trying to get more power to it. "Yeah, but I've never seen one," he said, "I'm not sure I even believe in them."

Iben stared at the window. He was no longer looking out into space. He was looking at the reflection in the glass. In the window, Iben could see a hawk-faced woman. Her blonde hair was in a tight ponytail and her naval uniform was immaculate. The reflection was saying something that Iben couldn't hear. It was the same words, over and over again.

Sandoval gave up on the war table and turned to the rest of the room. He looked at Iben, who was staring out the window. Sandoval floated over to the communications console. The frozen body of the comms officer was still strapped into their seat. He undid their restraints and let the body float free. He plugged the power unit into the console, trying to power it up.

He thought he saw something move in the reflection of the frozen console, but thought it was just the body of the comms officer. He had no luck getting the console to come online. Again he saw the reflection in the console and looked closer at it.

The reflection was of a woman's face. Her sharp features were gaunt and hollow. Her lips were moving, but he could not make out what she was saying. He could tell that it was the same words over and over again.

Iben could now hear a voice in his head. It was an authoritative woman's voice. His eyes were locked on the reflection in the window. The blonde, hawk-faced woman stared at him with black, empty eyes. The voice was repeating five names. Iben started to say them as well, not realizing it or knowing why: *"Camulus, Kara Mate, Kauraris, Kovus and Maher,"* he whispered.

"What was that?" Sandoval asked, turning to look at Iben. He pushed off of the console and floated over to his partner, "Hey Iben. Let's get going. We need to get back to *the Harvey*."

He reached out and touched Iben's shoulder. As if a puppet with its strings cut, Iben's pressure suit collapsed under his hand, with nothing inside.

"Iben!" Salvador yelled, shuffling through the other pressure suit and found that it was empty.

When he looked into the helmet, there was a reflection in the glass. It was Iben's face, as if he were standing behind Sandoval. The man turned but saw nothing. Looking back as quickly as zero gravity would allow, Sandoval saw Iben's face again. This time, the young man's mouth was moving, but Sandoval could not make out what was being said.

He clicked the channel switch on his radio. "Horrigan, Matthews come in," he said.

He received only static at first, which was not surprising considering they were at opposite ends of the broken, kilometer-long hull. After a moment, the static cleared.

"*Camulus...Kara Mate...*" came Horrigan's voice.

Sandoval looked confused for a moment. "What was that?" he asked, "Say again?"

"*Kauraris...Kovus...*"came the reply in Matthews' voice.

"Alright you two, get back to *the Harvey* and let's get out of here," he said. He slowly turned and pushed off the deck plating, towards the door.

As he floated through the air, the doors slid shut, trapping him inside.

"What the hells?" he said, trying to push them open. Without his tools, which were on the other side, opening them would be impossible.

He turned in the room, looking for another way out. Immediately, he was stopped by Iben. The young man was out of his pressure suit. His skin was pale, his eyes black and sunken, his lips purple. Sandoval tried to grab the young man but his hand passed right through him, as if he wasn't there.

"What in the Trinity?" he muttered. That was when he noticed the rest of them.

Even though their bodies were frozen in place at their stations, the bridge crew of the *Strife* were all standing behind Iben. One of them stepped forward. Her features were sharp, almost hawk-like. Her face was pale and gray, her eyes black as space. Her purple lips started to move, and so did the mouths of the rest of the crew.

"*Camulus,*" they all said in unison, "*Kara Mate, Kauraris, Kovus, Maher.*"

She peered into Sandoval's helmet, her eyes burrowing into his soul. He saw horrible images; people's souls being torn from their bodies, bodies being sucked into space or shredded by debris and explosions. They all flashed through his mind as the crew chanted the words, as if summoning something. Try as he might, he could not fight it. Her will was too strong.

His mouth started to stutter, "*C-C-Camulus...*" he said, not understanding why, "*Kara Mate...*" he continued, starting to feel cold on the inside, "*K-kauraris...*" he moaned, "*Kovus...*" he whispered, feeling himself slip away, "*Maher!*" he said in immense pain.

"*Strife!*" they all said, together.

Sandoval's pressure suit floated limp and empty on the bridge of the broken United Planets Dreadnaught *Strife*.

The ethereal form of Captain Jessica Summers floated to her command chair aboard the ghost ship. She looked at her crew as they all took their stations, and gave them orders that no one heard. Turning to the ghosts of Iben and Sandoval, she gave them a silent order. They both turned and passed through the doors, leaving the bridge.

The hull of the wrecked ship began to glow purple. A moment later, the spirit of the Dreadnaught lazily lumbered forward, leaving the broken wreckage of its physical form. It joined the other five ghost ships that hung silently in space. The former warships *Camulus*, *Kara Mate*, *Kauraris*, *Kovus and Maher*, all fell into formation behind the ghost Dreadnaught.

The six ships and their crews, were trapped in the mortal world. Singularity Spirits, created when the crew died while transitioning through or travelling within a singularity. They were angry and vengeful, and they would make anyone in their way suffer.

The physical wreck of the *Strife*, and now the hull of *the Harvey* continued to float, empty and powerless in the void, as the ghostly fleet navigated away.

Biographies

Jana Begovic

As far back as she can remember, Jana has been fascinated by storytelling. Her love of reading and writing propelled her toward studies of languages and literature resulting in B.A. degrees in English and German Languages and Literature, an M.A. Degree in Literary Criticism, as well as a B.Ed. Degree in English and Dramatic Arts.

Among her publications are an academic article published by Cambridge Scholars, UK, the novel *Poisonous Whispers*, poetry, short fiction, articles, art reviews, and blog posts featured in literary journals, such as *Ariel Chart*, *Chantwood*, the *Pangolin Review*, *Abstract*, *Canada Fashion Magazine* and *Authors Publish* (Facebook page).

Her short story, *Purveyors of Magic* will appear in the springtime edition of *Black Shamrock*.

Currently, she is working on a collection of children's stories and acting as a contributing editor/writer for *Ariel Chart* and *Canada Fashion Magazine*. She has been nominated for the 2019 Best of the Net and the PushCart Awards for a piece of non-fiction and a short story published in *Ariel Chart*.

She lives in Ottawa, Ontario and works for the Government of Canada as an education specialist in the field of military language training. She can be contacted via her Author Page at https://www.facebook.com/J.Damselfly/

Anna Blauveldt

Anna Blauveldt was born and raised in Fredericton, New Brunswick, and graduated with an Honours B.A. degree from the University of New Brunswick. She then moved to Ottawa to join the federal government and was fortunate to be appointed Canada's Ambassador to Iceland before leaving to pursue her next career as an author.

She subsequently completed the Post-Graduate Creative Writing Program of Humber College, Toronto and obtained an M.A. degree with Merit in Creative and Critical Writing from the University of Gloucestershire, UK, in 2019.

Anna's published works include,
- "Kat and the Meanies" - 2016, Under the Maple Tree Books (Atlanta USA, London UK, now defunct)
- "Irma" - 2019 anthology 'A Two-Four of Tales', Ottawa Independent Writers.
- "Released" - 2020 anthology 'Short Stories for a Long Year', Ottawa Independent Writers .
- "BFF" - 2022 anthology 'Conversations', Unleash Press (Ohio USA).

- "To Play At God" and "Ask Gloria" - Published in one volume, October 2021, Publerati, (Maine USA)
- and soon to be released "The Leavetaking" (2023)

Summer Breeze

Summer Breeze is an author, artist, and healer currently residing in Ottawa. Her *Wild Thing Gardens* are living proof that her fertile imagination is not limited to the written word. This free spirit can usually be found puttering amongst the flowers or dancing barefoot at the beach, connecting to the joy in life.

She has appeared in *Broken Keys Publishing's* Award-winning anthology, *Thin Places: The Ottawan Anthology*, with his short story, *The Lighthouse*.

Her poem *A Time of Darkness* has appeared in *Broken Keys Publishing's* 2022 Book of the Year, *Love & Catastrophē Poetrē*.

Jim Davies

Jim Davies is a cognitive scientist living in Ottawa and a member of the Lyngarde writer's group. His plays have been produced by *Push Push Theatre* in Atlanta, *Sock 'n' Buskin* in Ottawa, Chicago's *Otherworld Theatre Company*, *The Oak theatre* in Atlanta, and the *Critical Stage Company* in Kingston.

His poetry has appeared in *Bywords* literary magazine and *Altered Reality Magazine*. He is author of the serialized fiction series *Eve Pixiedrowner and the Micean Council*, an urban animal fantasy, and is author of the popular science books *Riveted: The Science of Why Jokes Make Us Laugh, Movies Make Us Cry, and Religion Makes Us Feel One with the Universe*, *Imagination: The Science of Your Mind's Greatest Power*, and *Being the Person Your Dog Thinks You Are: The Science of a Better You*.

Codi Jeffreys

Codi Jeffreys has been happily in radio for too many years to count and currently hosts her own Morning Show on Ottawa's *Lite 98.5-FM*. She also has recently taken on a part time gig as a Veterinary Assistant at Alta Vista Animal Hospital. Being that music and animals are her passions, this works well for her, radio and vet life. Her other hobbies include photography, reading, going on long nature walks, writing (hence adding to this wonderful compilation) and art.

Her poem *Hindsight is 20/20* has appeared in *Broken Keys Publishing's* 2022 Book of the Year, *Love & Catastrophē Poetrē*, and she has written the foreword for *Thin Places: The Ottawan Anthology*.

George Foster

George Foster is a retired Engineering Consultant for the Nuclear Power industry. He has written well over 600 procedures, program documents, training manuals and reports.

He is a member of the *North Grenville Writers Circle* and is trying hard to develop his own fiction voice and style. In the summer he can be found on the golf course, on his bike or on the river in his kayak. In the winter he hunkers down in the warmth of his living room to write, accompanied by his black lab Kimber and the family's pet Jenday Conure Lulu.

In addition to short stories George is working on a science fiction novel about a time machine built by Nikola Tesla.

He has appeared in *Broken Keys Publishing's* Award-winning anthology, *Thin Places: The Ottawan Anthology*, with his short story, *Belt Buckle*.

You can reach him at georgefoster34@hotmail.com

Matthew Lalonde

Matthew was born in Almonte, Ontario and raised in Ottawa. Reading in various formats; books, comic books e-books etc, has always been a past time of his, along with world building and writing. Sci-Fi to Fantasy to History, almost anything can tickle his reading bone. A self-described "hack," he has written many a short story for his own amusement, some of which even form a cohesive story or two. This is his first official submission to a project like this, and hey, it may even get printed! Could he still call himself a hack after that?

Other than reading and writing, music is his next biggest hobby, though he cannot play an instrument to save his life.

Other hobbies include, but are not limited to: Computer Games, Board and Card Games, collecting medieval hand weapons, Playing various tabletop RPG's, Eating food and sleeping. He is sure that there are more, but he can't think of them as of the writing of this bio.

He has appeared in *Broken Keys Publishing's* Award-winning anthology, *Thin Places: The Ottawan Anthology,* with his short story, *Y2K*.

Allan McCarville

Allan McCarville is a Stittsville author and researcher who has published a number of books in various genres, including historical fiction, fantasy adventure, and stories about the paranormal. Upon retiring from the federal government, he had the choice between working as a door greeter at a neighbourhood box store, or crafting stories. He believes writing is much more fun, although he admits he would have made more money as a door greeter. A complete listing of Allan McCarville's published works is available at www.allansbooks.com.

Emma Schuster

Emma Schuster is a twenty-year-old poet and Environment Studies student at the University of Waterloo. She is currently writing and working out of Ottawa. After discovering her love of poetry at eleven, she began to write and hasn't stopped since. Emma recently released a self-published poetry zine about her love for the city of Ottawa.

Sara Scally

Sara Scally is a third generation army brat and mother of three. When she is not writing she can be found hidden under a mountain of fabric and costumes and even as an adult loves to play pretend.

She has appeared in *Broken Keys Publishing's* Award-winning anthology, *Thin Places: The Ottawan Anthology*, with his short story, *Eye of the Beholder*.

Michel Weatherall

Author, Poet, Publisher, Printer, Imagination-weaver. A native of Ottawa, Michel Weatherall grew up as an army-brat living in Europe and Germany and has since travelled extensively.

Having over 35 years experience in the print/publishing industry, the transition to self-publishing was a natural step with his publication company, *Broken Keys Publishing & Press*.

Weatherall's current books in print are, *The Symbiot 30th Anniversary, The Nadia Edition, Necropolis, The Refuse Chronicles, Ngaro's Sojourney,* and *A Dark and Corner of My Soul (poetry)*.

His poem "This Burden I Bear" appeared in *This Could Be The Last Time: A Collection of Poems on Pandemics, Places, and Everything* (April 2020) (Apt613).

Other works have appeared in *Ariel Chart's International Journal* (the poems *"Sun & Moon," "This Burden I Bear," "Eleven's Silent Promise"* and the sci-fi short story *"Rupture,"* and several articles), as well as *The Indian Periodical* (*"Jacob's Darkness"*). His theological essay *"The Voice of Sophia"* has been published in American theologian Thomas Jay Oord's *"The Uncontrolling Love of God: An Open and Relational Account of Providence"* (2015).

Accolades and Awards include
- Winner of the 2020-21 Faces of Ottawa Awards Best Author
- 2021 Best of the Net Nominee for *"Purgation"*
- 2020-21 Parliamentary Poet Laureate Nominee
- 2020 Best of the Net Nominee for*"This Burden I Bear"*
- 2019 Pushcart Prize Nominee (Poetry),
- 2019 FEBE Awards Nominee for Creative Arts,
- 2019 CPACT Awards Nominee for Entertainment Excellence (Arts),
- 2018-19 Faces of Ottawa Awards Finalist for Favourite Author.